ROCK & ROLL

By

Khalil Murray

Copyright 2017 by The Equal Team Publications
Excerpt from Gossip Alley

Library of Congress Control Number: 2017954691
ISBN-978-0-692-96564-1

10 9 8 7 6 5 4 3 2 1

Published by:
The Equal Team Publications, LLC
Philadelphia, Pennsylvania
E-mail: TeTpublications@gmail.com

Dedication

This book is dedicated to my wife. Up or down, rich or broke, in jail or free, you continue to stand by my side. Baby, I love you, and I most definitely appreciate you.

Acknowledgements

Attempting the impossible is never an easy task. To be in jail, while doing so, is an even harder goal to achieve. The Equal Team Publications isn't an idea of mine to be alive momentarily. Over three decades ago, my brother, Bobby Sab, launched The Equal Team as a graffiti group. In honoring his legacy, I'm taking his vision many levels higher. I've made this prison cell an office, and with a lot of sacrifices and discipline, I've worked late into the night, and many mornings, I've chosen my typewriter over going to breakfast. In ten years, I've treated this time like I was overseas, studying in Mecca, or at one of these colleges, majoring in business.

In my prior novels, I chose to exclude an acknowledgement section, because I had few people that I felt should be mentioned. There is a story behind my first three books. The production of each one was far from easy. If you are reading this, and have purchased those books, I'm extremely grateful for your support. I put my best and my all into these stories for y'all.

You are about to read about one of my favorite characters in this 10-book series, and trust me, the wait for it was well worth it. When you're done, please share your review of the book on your social media pages, and on

Amazon, if that's how you purchased it. After Allah, my Creator, and Provider, my gratitude must go to my parents, Robert Murray, and Katrina Johnson. I am a borderline genius, because of their genes, and because of how I was raised by them. My love for reading came from my father's library, and my ability to chase my dreams as an author came from my mother's undying belief that I had it in me to do whatever I wanted with my life. So, to my parents, I am honored to be your son, and I hope that what I am doing as a publisher and author is providing you both with an immense amount of pride. I'm far from done. This chapter of being in jail is almost over for me, Insha Allah. What I'm about to do when I come home will be epic for our family.

To all my niggaz in jail, I appreciate the love and support. Y'all had my first book flying out of Black & Nobel back in 2014. To my family, your support is priceless. Knowing that I have some of y'all in my corner brings a different comfort to my heart. To the ones that won't even show me any social media love, much less, buy my books, don't be in my face when I get out there. Stay consistent with the corny shit.

If you somebody I don't know . . . thank you. Your book purchase is helping me pursue a dream of becoming an example for men in prison, and men on the street. A hustle is a hustle. It don't always have to be drugs, and a lot of dudes are struggling with abandoning that poisonous mindset. Sometimes, we just have to be around better people. In some cases, it might take jail, for a dude to reshape his focus on life. It's books for me. For you, it might be carpentry, real estate, music, computers, or driving 18-wheelers around the country. Progress requires sacrifice.

Evolve.

City of Secrets
10-book Series

Mr. and Mrs. Gunplay

Unbreak My Heart

Philadelphia Teardrops

Rock & Roll

Gossip Alley

Memories & Enemies

Wet Dreams

Philadelphia Wiretaps

Lookin' For Enemies

Philadelphia Nightmares

ROCK & ROLL

Chapter One

"So, what should I do, if I see Mommy somewhere?"

"What? Party, man, what kind of fuckin' question is that? You better try to blow that bitch head the fuck off..."

With a sigh, Party switched his cell phone to his opposite ear, as he flipped over on his bed, to his back. For a moment, Party stared blankly up at the ceiling fan above him, no longer paying any attention to the ranting his older brother was doing on the other end of his cell phone.

"... that bitch! Yo, I can't believe you just asked me some nut ass shit like that. Fuck that bitch over, Party. Shoot her in the fuckin' face as many times as you fuckin' can. It's on-sight wit' that bitch. Yo, you hear me?"

"Yeah, I hear you, but—"

"Man, it ain't no fuckin' buts, Party!"

"Sab, I'm not'chu!"Party snapped, sitting up in bed. Bottled up emotions began saluting his heart, as words buried deep down inside of his chest, since he had been a child, started to escape his lips."Ain't that what'chu wanna hear me say! There, I said it! I'm not'chu! That's what'chu wanna hear me say, right?! You happy, now?! You feel better?! Just 'cause I don't wanna kill Mommy, don't mean I don't hate her as much as you! But that's how you feel, though, right?!Ain't that what'chu told Uncle Sko yesterday?! Sab, he told me everything you said!"

"So, what?! Party, I ain't tell Uncle Sko shit different, than what I always tell you! Nigga, and stop fuckin' hollerin' at me! I ain't the fuckin' enemy . . . Mommy is!"

It was February 9th, 2013, thirty-seven minutes shy of it being midnight. The dark sky was clear, except for the bright display of a full, shimmering moon. The city of Philadelphia had just recovered from one of its coldest days, and according to local, weather experts, no relief was to be seen in the week to come.

For Party, whose real name was Pierre Anderson Jr., the cold temperature felt eerily appropriate. Party's life had been turned upside down, and inside out, on a cold, rainy day. Cold and rainy days were when Party was emotionally vulnerable the most. Only the people closest to him were aware of this.

"Party, do you want Mommy to do to you, what she got done to Daddy?"

"No."

"Alright, well, you gotta act like it, then, man. Party, this shit ain't no game. You Daddy second comin', Party. Don't'chu see him when you look in the mirror? You look just like him. Everybody say it."

"I know."

"Party, man, we owe it to Daddy, to get Mommy back. It's up to us. Us, Party. Nobody else. I know you don't like how we been livin' our lives the last ten years."

Party caught a falling teardrop with his left hand.

"Party, I don't either. This the cards we been dealt, though. Like, and trust me, I know more than anybody else, that all this nut ass shit is a lot for you to have on your shoulders at the age of eighteen, but–Like, what other options we got, Party? We can't go to the cops. We definitely not givin' Mommy Daddy fuckin' money. Party, we talked about this shit a million fuckin' times, man. I

2

keep tellin' you what it's gon' come down to. Our lives ain't gon' never be normal again, until we find Mommy, and rock her crazy ass."

"You think she still might be in Philly?"

"I doubt it, but, then, like, who knows? That's why you gotta keep ya eyes open, and be the fuck on point at all times out there, Party. This shit not just about'chu not bein' me. Party, Mommy know she ain't gotta fuckin' snowball chance in Hell, if she ever cross my fuckin' path. If she cross yours, and you don't park her ass, her whole angle gon' be to use you as leverage to get Daddy money from me. Party, she gon' torture you. I told you what they sayin' she did to that ol'head she was just fuckin' wit'. She gon' have you somewhere, where ain't nobody gon' be able to hear ya screams. She gon' be doin' all that voodoo shit on you 'n all'lat. And even if I give her Daddy money, she still gon' kill you, Party. So, like, if you ain't really ready to put on some fuckin' war paint, then go back to Boston wit' Uncle Sko, until I come home, before Mommy make the score two to nothin'."

With a sigh, Party slammed his fist into one of his bed pillows, before stretching his body across the middle of his bed. Party's thoughts were starting to race. Wherever his mother was, he wanted her to stay there. Just talking about a potential encounter with her had him suddenly feeling anxious, and uncomfortable.

"Party, man, you begged me to let'chu come back to Philly for the last ten years. You got what'chu been askin' me for. Help me keep Daddy legacy goin', Party. Show me this wasn't a mistake, by lettin' you come back. Party, I want'chu to show Mommy what'chu made of."

"I am," Party promised, feeling inspired by his older brother's words and sentiments. Thoughts of his father brought along emotions of anger and sadness, causing teardrops of frustration to start pouring from his eyes." I been waitin' for this moment, since I was eight, Sab. I ain't never goin' back to Boston. You the one that made that decision for me to go stay wit' Uncle Sko, not me. Sab, that shit was like fuckin' boot camp."

"Yeah, but look what it did for you, though. Party, if you apply just some of that shit you learned in Boston from Uncle Sko, and pivot off that shit in Philly, Party, Mommy, or nobody else, won't be able to fuck wit'chu. Not only that, but'chu got access to anything you want."

"I know."

"Alright, man, look, let's finish this conversation another time. I gotta call Breen, and make sure she still comin' up here tomorrow."

"She told me she was when I talked to her earlier."

"Yeah, but, I'm tryna get my celly a visit, too, though. I'm tryna'get Breen to bring his babymom 'n son up."

"Sab?"

"Yo?"

"They still gon' let'chu go next year?"

"Hopefully. My minimum February twenty-fourth. I ain't got no write-ups, so it shouldn't be no reason why these mu'fuckers don't gimme the green light."

"Is what Uncle Sko told me true?"

"What he say?"

"That, if one of them guards catch you in there wit' that cell phone, it's gon' automatically mess up ya chances of comin' home."

"Man, tell Uncle Sko to fall back."

"Will it, though?"

"Party, let me worry about that. Everything cool. Trust me, I'm comin' home, alright? Ay, did Breen give you ya own set of keys to the hair salon; like I told her to?"

"Yeah, I got 'em right here in my pocket."

"Alright, well, look, I'ma holla at'chu tomorrow, alright?"

"Alright."

"Alright, man, I love you."

"Love you, too."

Ten years earlier . . .

January 7th, 2002

8:47 p.m.

Something.

Wrong.

"Party, they killed Daddy!"

After his crippling confession, Sab pulled the rear passenger door to his car shut, then frantically began to unbuckle Party's seatbelt. Sab's clothes were drenched from the rain, and his eyes were wet with tears.

"Mommy did it. It was Mommy. Party, she . . . That bitch got Daddy kidnapped, and then they . . ."

The moment his older brother's uncontrollable sobbing started, seemed more defining for Party, than the news his older brother had just given him about their father's fate. Party was only eight-years-old, so his young mind wasn't quite able to grasp the reality, or the sheer magnitude of what his older brother had just revealed to him. Due to this lack of comprehension, Party only became emotional, and also began to cry, because his older brother was himself.

Party was the youngest of two children. His brother, Baseer, who everyone called, 'Sab', was ten years his senior. Party was their father's exact replica; just a tinier version, and minus the beard. Like their father, Party was also allergic to cats, and seafood, and he loved butter pecan, ice cream. It was Sab, who had their mother's looks. Sab had her green eyes, the same light complexion, and he even had a sprinkle of freckles on both cheeks, and on the tip of his nose.

Pierre Anderson Sr., Party and Sab's father, was the combination of a mother from Portugal, and an African American father from New Orleans. His parents had stumbled upon love at a coffee shop in Montreal, Canada. Pierre was born in Montreal, but had been raised in New Orleans, where, he himself, had found love, during his senior year of high school. In his mid-twenties, Pierre had come to the decision that he wanted him and his then-pregnant wife, to move to the city of Philadelphia, where he had an older brother. The move had also been inspired by Pierre's underworld ties to an Italian, drug kingpin, by the name of Salvatore Masino. With Salvatore Masino's backing, it had only taken Pierre one year to establish himself in the streets of Philadelphia. It had taken him an additional three years to proclaim himself a self-made millionaire. However, while the drug trade had been generous to Pierre, life at home with his wife had become a living hell.

Party and Sab's mother had a soul that was darker than the mouth of a train tunnel. She was 'Revlon' beautiful, but owned a wicked personality that was 'Donkey Kong' ugly. Her name was Victoria Beauvais, and Party was afraid of her.

Sab hated everything about her.

He even hated that they looked alike.

Victoria Beauvais practiced witchcraft. It was her religion, and a strong piece of her family's heritage. In New Orleans, her family roots were legendary. She had two sets of twin aunts, who specialized in all kinds of black magic spells. These four aunts, who were the younger sisters of Victoria's father, had invested a lot of their lives into teaching Victoria everything that had been taught to them. It had been their older brother's dying wish. Pierre had been Victoria's first project. In her possession, Victoria had intoxicating perfume that, if smelled once by any man, the fragrance would leave Victoria in total control of that man's thinking, and his decisions, so long as that man and Victoria had sex. To simply inhale the aroma, would only leave a man feeling light-headed, and disoriented, hours afterwards.

During the summer of 1999, the decades-long spell Victoria had had over Pierre had become lifted. Ironically, it had been by Victoria's very own undoing. She had contracted an STD from someone else, but in her rage, had immediately placed the blame on her husband. The problem was, after an emergency visit to a nearby health clinic, it was quickly revealed that Pierre was actually STD-free. Following a toxic war of words, Pierre had moved out of their home, and the very next day, had hired a divorce attorney.

It was Party, who had suffered the most from his father's absence at home. His mother, who had seemed to always find reasons why he needed to be punished, or chastised, and she was always upset and angry. Even more confusing to Party, was what his mother had done to their basement. She had transformed it into her own personal, voodoo cavern. On all of their basement's walls, there was unreadable, cryptic writing, and all sorts of drawings, ranging in all colors, which glowed, and sometimes, appeared to move, whenever the lights were off. The floor of the basement was stained with blood. There were animals of all sizes locked in cages. Party had, through crying eyes, watched as his mother drunk blood of exotic animals he had never seen before. Sometimes, she would bathe naked in blood, after many of her animal sacrifices. Like always, after all of these bizarre incidents, Party's mother would grab him violently by the face, and threaten him with certain death, if his lips were to ever utter one single word of what he had been witnessing at home, to his father, Sab, his school teachers, or anyone else.

Sab had moved out of their house a week after his father had left. He was his father's second-in-command, and at the young age of seventeen, had seen, and touched, more money than a bank teller ever would.

Something.

Wrong.

At the ringing of his cell phone, Sab freed Party from his embrace, then ordered his girlfriend, who was sitting behind the steering wheel of his silver, Dodge Intrepid, to kill the engine on the car. Sighing, Sab took a moment to wipe the teardrops from his face. His girlfriend watched him through the rearview mirror. Party's watery eyes were staring at Sab's ringing cell phone.

"That's her?"

Sab nodded his head at his girlfriend as he raised his cell phone up to his ear. For emotional strength, Sab put Party beneath the wing of his left arm, then answered their mother's call. Sab met his girlfriend's eyes in his rearview mirror.

"Hello?"

"Mom—Mommy, I—I only got six hundred and eighty-five thousand right now. It was all I could—That's all I could get together that fast."

"And what the fuck am I supposed to do with that, Sab?! Huh?! Tell me that, mother fucker?!"

Victoria Beauvais had a voice that could scare a ghost. It was always kept at a few levels above a whisper, and sounded like something that would come out of the mouth of a female zombie in a horror film. No feelings or sensitivity was ever attached to it. Victoria Beauvais' voice was lifeless and dark; like her heart.

"Mommy, man, why you doin' this to us?"

"Sab, do you wanna see your father the fuck alive again, or what?"

"Yeah."

"Okay, well, then, I advise you to end the fuckin' questions. Get me what I asked for."

"Can I talk to Daddy again?"

"Once was enough. And I want the address to that fuckin' house, too."

"What house?"

"Sab, don't play with my fuckin' intelligence, okay? Not tonight. I been doin' this shit long before you was born. You and I both know damn well what fuckin' house I'm talkin' the fuck about."

Pierre Anderson Sr. owned a house in Gladwyne, Pennsylvania, that had a little over twenty million dollars in cash in its guest bedroom. The money was hidden in the drop-ceiling, in the denomination of one hundred dollar bills. The money was being kept inside of fifteen, leather, Fendi suitcases. Only Sab knew where this house was located. Anybody, who was somebody, knew about the role that Sab played in his father's drug enterprise. Sab had more intelligence of what was actually going on in the streets of Philadelphia, than some DEA agents, who had been employed by the government, far longer than Sab had been alive. Both Sab, and his girlfriend of three and a half years, held intricate positions in Sab's father's drug dynasty. The two of them were money couriers for him. Both of them were equipped with fake driver's licenses, and had access to dozens of cars. Sab and his girlfriend also had Sab's father's permission, to shoot at anyone, who either of them perceived to be a potential threat. Up until now, nothing had ever arisen, where it had called for either one of them to respond with any kind of deadly force.

Until.

Now.

"Mommy, I'ma have everything you want in an hour."

"Thirty fuckin' minutes, Sab. Thirty fuckin' minutes. And if you try anything slick, I'm sendin' somebody after your little brother."

"That's—But—He—Mommy, he ya son, though."

"I can always have another one. And don't think I don't know about Sabreena pickin' Party up from the neighbor's house. Make sure you let that bitch know, if she interfere with my fuckin' business ever again, she gon' have hell to pay."

Before Sab could respond to his mother's cold and insensitive threats, she abruptly ended their call. The clock was ticking now.

"Sab, what she say?"

Sab looked at his girlfriend with sadness brushing across the contours of his facial features. Her question had brought fresh tears to his eyes. Those tears began spilling as he thought about his mother's threats. He now feared for his little brother and girlfriend. The pressure of what was happening had him feeling like the weight of the world was on his shoulders, and it was a burden like any he had ever experienced.

"Sab, what she–"

"If I don't give her what she asked for, in thirty minutes, she gon' send somebody for Party."

"Well, she can forget that, 'cause he with us now."

"She already know that. She wanna know where my dad house at, too."

"Which one?"

"Breen, which one you think? The one out Gladwyne."

"So, what we gon' do, then?"

Sab looked down at his left wrist, checking the time on his watch. He had twenty-seven minutes to meet his mother's demands.

"You givin' her what she want?"

"What? Fuck no . . . Breen, I'ma give this bitch hell. Her, and whoever she got ridin' wit' 'er."

"And you sure she killed y'all dad already?"

"When I just asked her to let me talk to him again, she wouldn't let me."

"Yeah, but that don't mean–"

"Breen, he dead. I can feel it. He dead. I can feel that shit in my fuckin' heart, man."

"This is so crazy. Oh, my God. I can't believe this is really happening right now, Sab."

"Look, this what we gon' do."

For a little over ten minutes, Party sat quietly, listening attentively, as Sab and his girlfriend, planned, and went over several different scenarios, until they both finally agreed on an option that seemed to be less difficult, than all of the rest. While Sab and his girlfriend had been talking, it had begun to rain a lot harder. The raindrops had gotten heavier. They were beating on the roof of Sab's car with a steadier rhythm, than before. Sab's car was parked at the corner of 5th and Morris, in South Philadelphia. His girlfriend's white, Mazda 929, was directly across the street, parked in front of a Cambodian-owned, laundromat.

"Party, I'ma need'ju to grow up real fast," Sab insisted gently, while hugging his little brother's body as tight as he possibly could. His teardrops were spilling down into his little brother's low-cut, curly hair." It's a lot of stuff goin' on right now, Party. Crazy stuff. Stuff that'chu probably won't be able to really understand, until you get older. Party, I had to, um, get Breen to pick you up from Ms. Lindy house, 'cause Mommy got somethin' bad done to Daddy, and I wasn't tryna let the same thing happen to you. Mommy got Daddy kidnapped, Party. She want Daddy money, and she wanna know where Daddy new house at."

"The real big one that Daddy made me keep a secret about?"

"Yeah, Party, that one. That's what me 'n her was just talkin' about. I was gon' give her the money, but when she called me earlier, and she let me talk to Daddy, Daddy told me don't give Mommy nothin'. Daddy told me Mommy and her friends was gon' kill him anyway. You understand what I'm sayin'?It's not that I didn't wanna help Daddy, alright?"

Party truly didn't understand what was going on, but he still nodded his head anyway. The only thing clear to him, was that his little heart had him suddenly feeling desperate to see his father unlike ever before. After another hug, more tighter this time, Sab released Party from his embrace, and left the car. In Sab's absence, his girlfriend cried loud and hard.

So did Party.

Together, their crying was a sad duet. It was melodic, yet dynamically sympathetic. At times, Party's crying had gotten so uncontrollable, it sometimes began to sound like he was hyperventilating. For that reason, Sab's girlfriend urged Party to join her up front in the driver's seat.

When Sab returned, he got back into his car with the same silent aura he had left with. He had changed out of the wet clothes he had been wearing, and now had on a black, two-piece, rain suit. In his left hand, he was clutching the straps of a large duffel bag. In his right, he was gripping the handle of an Italian-made, automatic shotgun. His facial expression was murderous as he tossed the duffel bag over his shoulder into the bag seat. He could feel his girlfriend and Party's eyes watching his every move. Their attention inspired him not to let one single tear escape his eyes. In their eyes, he had to be brave.

Fearless.

Fearsome.

Sab dug deep down within himself, tapping into the strength that he knew he was going to need to outthink his mother. He was determined to avenge his father's death.

"Breen, we gotta go to the park on Fourth and Ellsworth."

"The dog park?"

Sab nodded as he leaned over and removed Party from his girlfriend's lap. Once Party was settled on his, Sab turned his attention to his girlfriend.

"She called me again."

"And said what?"

"She want me to go to the park on Fourth and Ellsworth. She want me to come alone, and to call her when I get there."

"But–"

"Look, we still stickin' to the same plan. Manny Yunk and Nacky on their way. They gon' meet us there."

Sabreena wiped her eyes and face clean of her tears, then started Sab's car. Fresh tears quickly replaced old ones as she cut on the headlights and windshield wipers, and pulled out of the parking space.

"We switchin' cars, too."

"Okay."

"Go to the Escalade."

"Which one?"

"Where you leave the black one yesterday?"

"Fourth and Dickinson. The white one around the corner, on Seventh street."

"Naw, go to the black one. For this shit, I want us to be inside somethin' bulletproof. Ain't no tellin' what might happen."

In war . . .

The wise shall prosper.

◦◯◦

9:59 p.m.

Never.

Fight.

Alone.

"Breen , pull over right there."

Obeying Sab's instructions, his girlfriend tapped the brakes on the black Escalade and pulled the SUV over to the northeast corner of 4th and Washington. It was still raining, but it had slowed down to a light drizzle.

"Alright, go 'head, Yunk. What'chu was sayin'?"

13

"Pay attention to that fuckin' blue, mini-van. This shit been circling that playground, since me 'n Nacky pulled up. Watch that shit turn up Fifth Street when it get to the corner."

Sab switched his cell phone to his opposite ear, and after leaning back, he focused all of his attention on the blue, mini-van, traveling west up Ellsworth Street. The windows on the mini-van were tinted, preventing Sab from seeing who was inside of it. Like his father's friend had predicted, the mini-van made a right turn at the corner of 5th and Ellsworth.

"Now, watch that shit make another right when it get up to Washington Avenue. Then, when it get down to Fourth, it's gon' make another one, right there in front of you. It's just doing circles. Young'n, that's them. It's ya call, though. Me and Nacky waitin' on you."

"Hold up, Yunk. Let me see what this shit do."

Again, like his father's friend had predicted, Sab witnessed the mini-van make a right turn as soon as it reached Washington Avenue. It was moving at a snail's pace, going no more than five miles an hour. Sab was mad that he couldn't see who was driving. The closer the mini-van got, the hotter Sab could feel his blood getting inside of his veins. The hand holding his cell phone against his ear had begun to shake uncontrollably.

"Yunk, y'all ready?"

"No question, young'n."

A second after Sab and his father's friend ended their call, Sab's mother called. At that same second, as Sab was accepting his mother's call, he gave his girlfriend a quick order to drive out into the middle of the 4th and Washington intersection, to cut off the blue, mini-van.

"Mommy?"

"Sab, my fuckin' patience is running out. Where the fuck are you?"

"Mommy, shut the fuck up!" Sab snapped, glaring at the windshield of the mini-van. His heart was doing flip-flops in his chest as he cracked the Escalade's passenger door, and dropped the heavy duffel bag down to the rain-wet street. "I got everything you fuckin' asked for! I know you ain't in this van! So, tell whoever drivin' this nut ass shit, to get the fuck out and get that shit! The fuckin' bag right there, in front of 'em!"

"Sab, how stupid do you think I am?"

"And the address to Daddy house in the bag, too!"

"Why are you suddenly so excited. It's a tell-tale sign, Sab."

By no means was Victoria Beauvais a dumb woman. She was as innovative, and ingenious, as she was evil. She had been planning her ex-husband's kidnapping for months. His schedule had become hers; so had Sab's and his girlfriend's. She had been able to stay several steps ahead of them all, because she had someone close to them feeding her information. That person was behind the steering wheel of the mini-van.

"Sab, I'm there, but I'm not in that van. This should be fun to watch."

The comment came from Sab's mother, just as Sab's girlfriend was reversing the Cadillac Escalade away from the duffel bag, and the mini-van. Sab's girlfriend stopped, once she was enough feet away from the mini-van, for her and Sab to watch it closely.

"Sab, I knew you couldn't be trusted. I know that Escalade is bulletproof. I'm the bitch who suggested it to your father. Sab, the van is a decoy. The driver is, too. And I seriously doubt that what I asked for is in that fuckin' duffel bag. Your father will never get a proper funeral. Tell your girlfriend to get her lies together."

As soon as the driver of the mini-van got out, and made an attempt for the duffel bag, he realized his grave mistake.

Manny Yunk and Nacky came running out of the 4th and Ellsworth park, pointing their assault rifles at him.

Sab frowned when his mother began to laugh wickedly on the other of his cell phone. This confirmed that she was definitely somewhere nearby. Sab watched as the driver of the mini-van slowly began to unpeel his ski-mask, as he made his exit from the Escalade with his automatic shotgun, leaving his cell phone behind. Party was observing the entire scene unfold from the backseat of the bulletproof Escalade. It was when Sab's girlfriend also exited the truck, that Party hurriedly unbuckled his seatbelt and climbed up to the front, wanting to only get a better look at what was happening. He also wanted to see the face of the man, removing his ski-mask. Party could hear his mother's maniacal laughter coming from his older brother's cell phone, as it laid face-up in the passenger's seat.

Once the driver of the mini-van was done pulling off his ski-mask, Sab and his girlfriend had two totally different reactions. Sab's girlfriend lowered her gun and immediately began to sob hysterically. Sab, however, had a disgusted look on his face as he kept his shotgun aimed at the unmasked man's chest. Manny Yunk and Nacky both began to back away, lowering their assault rifles. They both had disappointed expressions on their faces.

"Sab, man, I'm–Breen? Breen? Yo, I'm–I'm sorry."

It was an apology that blurred Sab's eyes with angry tears. Standing there, beneath the drizzling rain, and remarkably, no traffic was coming from either direction on Washington Avenue, or down 4th Street. Sab's girlfriend was crying beside him, seemingly wanting to offer an apology of her own as Sab leveled his automatic shotgun at the face of his girlfriend's identical twin brother. Sab squeezed the trigger, and the roar of the powerful shotgun caused Manny Yunk to slow up his black, Mercedes- Benz, as he drove across the 5th and Ellsworth intersection, going west. When her twin brother's body fell lifeless to the street, Sab's girlfriend turned her back and ran to the Escalade, and shut the door behind her. Her and Sab were both internally hating, but shocked, at the power and manipulation of Sab's mother's dark spells. As he backed away to the passenger side, of the Escalade, Sab looked around, wondering where his mother might be. She had assumed correctly. The duffel bag beside his girlfriend's brother's dead body contained nothing of value. It was stuffed with broken pieces of dry-wall, sheetrock, and some old doorknobs.

Sab grabbed the duffel bag, got back into the Escalade, and slammed the door in frustration. Still sobbing uncontrollably, his girlfriend shifted the SUV into drive and sped east down Washington Avenue, heading for the I-95 expressway. Her eyes kept returning to the rearview mirror, horrified at the sight of her twin brother blocks behind her, dead in the street. She was devastated to her core by his betrayal, and at witnessing her boyfriend bring his life to a quick end. Their parents could never learn the truth.

Sighing restlessly, Party blinked away the ten-year-old memory and sat up in bed. He wasn't quite certain that his decision to come back to Philadelphia was still a smart one.

After ten years of craving the day he would finally be back in Philadelphia, Party was feeling disappointed in it, now that the long-awaited day had arrived. The only things that had met his expectations, were the gifts his brother and girlfriend had purchased for him. Outside, he had an icy-gray, 2013 Range Rover Sport. The truck was bulletproof. The three-story house he was in, looked like something out of an Architectural Digest magazine. In the master bedroom, hiding behind the gigantic, flat-screen TV, there was a safe built into the wall, holding one hundred thousand dollars in cash, four Glock 40s, and a collection of expensive watches, all once worn by Party's father himself. Tonight, the only item Party had removed from the safe, was the automatic shotgun Sab had used to kill his girlfriend's twin brother. The gun had become a trophy for Sab.

Sab was currently at an upstate prison, serving two to four years, on an unrelated drug charge. He had gotten arrested with seventy-five bundles of heroin, while dropping the drugs off to an associate of his in West Philadelphia.

"Maybe, I should've listened to Uncle Sko,"Party thought, after closing his eyes and laying back down. Slowly inhaling through his nostrils, he flexed the fingers of his right hand around the pistol-gripped handle of his older brother's automatic shotgun. "I should've just went to college. At least, I could've lost my virginity there. Probably would've been meetin' all kinds of girls. From all over, too. Wouldn't be worryin' about Mommy findin' me. My life suck. I'm an eighteen-year-old virgin. Gotta show Sab he can count on me, until he come home. If I kill Mommy, before he get out, he'll really be proud of me."

Wishes.

Chapter Two

"Party, all of them nice. I can't see you not gettin' along with any of them."

"Just 'cause they all cool wit'chu, don't mean they gon' be the same way wit' me."

"Well, listen, all I can say to that, is this... fire whoever you don't like, Party. At the end of the day, that's your hair salon."

Party was sitting in his Range Rover, in front of his hair salon, listening to his older brother's girlfriend, as she told him all about his employees. While holding his cell phone to his ear, and listening to her talk, Party was studying his surroundings. He felt nervous.

It was a Tuesday morning, February 10th. Blustery winds were ruling the streets of Philadelphia. Above, the sky was gloomy and gray, and had an appearance of preparing to unleash a downpour of raindrops at any moment. Like the days prior, the dawn had begun, without the temperatures climbing no higher than the single digits.

"Breen, what time they usually be openin' up?"

"Well, Ashley, the one I told you manage the salon, she, um, usually get there first, and she opens up. Why? Wait... what'chu forgot the keys?"

"Naw, I got 'em right here."

"Bye, boy. Party, what'chu waitin' for? Go open up your barber shop. The salon, too. That's your business. Open it."

"Can I ask you somethin', Breen?"

"What?"

"If I see my mom somewhere, what should I do?"

Party heard his brother's girlfriend release an uncomfortable sigh on the other end of his cell phone. The night he had lost his father, she had suffered a lost herself.

"Party, I think you need to have this discussion with Sab."

"Did already."

"And what he say?"

"Take a guess."

Silence.

"Could you do that to ya own mom, Breen?"

"Party, the real question is, can you? Or better yet, will you? You already know how I feel about your mom. And we both know how Sab feel. Now, it all comes down to how you feel, Party."

"I hate her, too, Breen."

"Yeah, but, Party, having hate in your heart for her might not be enough when the time come for you to face her. How you feel, and what you ultimately do when, and if that moment come, is what me and Sab is concerned about, Party. You not little no more."

Party was on the verge of tears as he stared through his windshield down Marshall Street. He was pondering over the equations his brother's girlfriend had brought to light, and it was then that he realized something about himself that was causing him to feel shame. He was indeed his older brother's opposite. Even with knowing that his mother was solely responsible for his father's death, his heart still wouldn't allow him to shoot his mother in the face, or for that matter, even pull out a gun on her.

"Your mom don't want'chu to enjoy life, Party. She evil. I know it's not as simple as I'm probably makin' it sound, but let'cha knew life distract you from your old one. Put some miles on that Range Rover. Get familiar with Philly again. Party, go sight-seeing. Tear the mall down. You in control of ya own destiny now, Party. Live. You don't have ya uncle in ya ear no more, tellin' you what you can, and cannot do. Party, worry about ya mother another day. For today, do you. Be an eighteen-year-old. Flirt with some girls in the salon when they come in."

"Breen, you my favorite sister-in-law."

"Boy, I'm ya only sister-in-law. Shut up."

"Yeah, I know, but, like, if I did have another one, I'd make her feel like she was my step-sister-in-law. All the time, too."

Party and his brother's girlfriend shared a long and hearty laugh. It was another one of their many bonding moments, which, for Party, had come at a perfect time. The nervousness he had been feeling had gone away.

"Thanks, Breen."

"For what?"

"That laugh. For the pep-talk, too. I really needed that."

"Just return the favor when I look like I need one."

"I will."

"Alright, well, call me, if there's any problems at the shop, okay?"

"Alright."

"Party?"

"Huh?"

"Live."

"I am."

Party sat his cell phone in the cup holder of his truck's center console, then looked out of every window on his Range Rover, getting another good look at his surroundings. His barbershop was in North Philadelphia. It was located on the driver's side of Marshall Street, between Girard Avenue and Popular Street. On both sides of the block, there were numerous businesses. The establishments ranged from hair product stores, to day care centers, a breakfast store, and a nail salon, and down at the bottom of the block, there was a public assistance office. Feeling comfortable with his survey, Party pocketed his cell phone, then hopped out of his truck feeling excited. He took a moment to admire the awning, hanging above the large windows of his barber shop.

In white, cursive-lettering, on a long, burgundy awning, it read, 'Party's Hairshow'. In a smaller caption, the barber shop's phone number, address, and its business website, were all imprinted in the same lettering. Beneath the burgundy awning, there were two large, glass-fronts. Above the awning, there were two, bedroom windows, belonging to the one-bedroom apartment, that sat above the barber shop.

"Who—Who—Who you—Who you is?"

With his question, the chubby, black man, who was wearing a black patch over his right eye, stepped beside Party, and after blowing over the rim of his styrofoam cup of coffee, he joined Party in looking at the front of his barber shop. Quickly feeling uncomfortable with the one-eyed stranger's closeness, Party moved away from him and walked over to his barber shop's front door.

"You—You wanna get—g—get a hair—A haircut?"

As soon as Party figured out which keys went where, he hurriedly unlocked the all-glass door, and let himself into his barber shop. He was hoping to get away from the biting cold air, and the annoying stranger. Unfortunately, he was followed by the stuttering man, who he was suddenly feeling desperate to get away from.

"Every—Ev—Everybody call me St—St—St—Stutter Man."

In awe of the interior of his barber shop, Party continued ignoring the strange man, and took a few steps further into his barber shop and flipped up a light switch.

He was beyond impressed. Party's face slowly began to produce a proud smile. Seeing Party's smile, the man with the eye patch came and stood beside Party and started to smile too.

"Who–Who you–you is?"

"Party."

"Oh–Ohhhhhhh, sh–shiiiiit."

Party's barber shop had the appearance of style, finesse, and professionalism. The building was divided into two sections, and was actually a unisex salon. Its front area, which was dedicated to its male clientele, was close to possessing all of the electronic amenities any man could ever hope to have. There were flat-screen TVs, an iPod dock, that had a vast range of music stored in it, and several entertainment games, like Wii, a Kinect, and the latest PlayStation, that were all stored behind the reception counter. There were large mirrors, showing reflections from every wall. At the rear wall, beside the four hair-wash sinks, there was a soda machine, and a candy machine. In total, there were four barber stations. Above each one, hung a black, ceiling fan. Each ceiling fan had a gold trimming, and could be powered on or off, by the use of a tiny remote control, usually kept in the possession of the barbers. The floors of the barber shop were cut from Peruvian trees, and had the gloss of continued care, and maintenance. Across from the barber stations, there was a line of black, leather-padded chairs, for waiting clients.

In the rear of the barber shop, a small hallway, where there were three, small bathrooms, led to the hair salon. The floor of this hallway was black, Pergo tiles, and the walls of the hallway were colored with white, Ralph Lauren paint. The doors on the three bathrooms shared the same color.

The door to the hair salon was a soft pink, and its doorknob was gold-finished. On the center of the pink door, posted with four, pink thumbtacks, was a white sign with fancy, pink-lettering, that read, 'No Boys Allowed'.

Like the barber shop, the hair salon also had the texture of hardwood floors. There were also four stylist chairs as well. The wall opposite these four stations had a humongous, flat screen TV, and a tall bookcase, standing beside it. The hair salon's rear wall was the back for a large, towel rack, four hair washing sinks, and several hair dryers. The ceiling was adorned with similar ceiling fans like the barber shop. The front wall of the hair salon was a spotless, floor-to-ceiling mirror, and in front of it were eight, pink, leather-padded chairs, for waiting clients.

Done with touring his unisex salon, it was twenty-one minutes later, and Party and Stutter Man were talking and joking with one another, as if they had known each other for several years.

"Oh–Ohhhhhh, sh–shiiiiiit."

"What?"

"M–M–Maaannnnn, h–h–h–here c–come C–C–Camille."

Party was too determined to take down the high score on the video game he was sitting in front of, to look away. He had been glued to the video game, since inserting his first five dollar bill.

"Party, I–I'll–M–Mannnnn, I'll–I'll ssssuck a f–fart outta her b–b–butthole."

The comment took Party completely by surprise, and sent him into a fit of laughter that had tears coming to his eyes. It was the thought of actually sucking a fart out of someone's butt that had him nearly choking, and nearly toppling off of the stool he was sitting on. He had never in his life heard such a thing. It was unthinkable. Nasty. The funniest thing Party had ever heard in his entire life. Still laughing, while still desperately trying not to lose his chance for the high score on the video game, Party craned his neck around Stutter Man's big shoulder, so he could get a look at who Stutter Man was speaking so freakishly about.

"Damn," Party thought, no longer laughing, as his eyes took in the sight of the sexy female, who had just stepped out of a white, Nissan Murano. Her femininity quickly began to make his virginity howl beneath his skin, and he hadn't even laid eyes on her face yet. "Her body crazy. Look at her ass. I wonder which one . . ."

To Stutter Man's humor, Party dipped back behind the video game the moment Camille turned from her jeep, and started walking towards the barber shop's front door.

"And–And . . . she allllways be smellin' g–good, P–Party."

"Go open the door for her."

"You go."

"Naw, man. Go 'head."

"You–M–Mannnnn, is you scared of p–p–pussy?"

"No."

Stutter Man gave Party a judging look, then, with a mischievous smile on his face, he hurried by all of the barber stations, until he reached the first one. There, Stutter Man pulled open a drawer and stuck his hand inside of it. Shortly after, a buzzing sound could be heard, prompting Camille to pull at the door.

"P–Party, watch h–h–how she walk."

Party didn't dare. Instead, he shifted nervously on the wooden stool and stared more intently at the game he was playing.

"What'chu just say, Stutter Man? I know you ain't just say somethin' smart about me?"

"I sssaid, g–good mor–m–mornin', C–Camille."

"You lyin'."

"Y–Yessss, I d–did. H–How–H–How you g–g–gonna tell me?"

"Whateva . . . who that back there, playin' the game?"

Party cringed, and stopped breathing. He thought about running back to the hair salon, or pretending that he needed to use the bathroom, but his legs refused to obey him. His palms suddenly became sweaty.

"Razor, that's you back there?"

"N–No, SSStupid. That's P–Party."

"Boy, call me stupid again. You lyin'. It is not."

"Go–G–Go see, then. P–P–Party, p–pull ya d–d–dick out on her."

"Stutter Man, make me smack ya mu'fuckin' ass up in here this mornin'!"

Party's heartbeat sped up, matching the quickly approaching footsteps. Retreating to the hair salon, or the bathroom, was still weighing heavily on his mind, but his legs still wouldn't obey him for some unknown reason. He had no experience when it came to socializing with people he didn't know; especially females. He had lived a sheltered life, the entire ten years he had stayed in Boston with his uncle. His uncle had home-schooled him, and had always taken the threat of Party potentially being found by his mother very seriously. If it hadn't been for watching TV, and going on the internet, Party would have been clueless to what was going on in the real world.

The closer Camille got to Party, the faster Party's heart sped up. He could smell Camille's perfume. It was drifting in the air, bringing the scent of candy, flowers, and strawberries. The aroma was disturbing Party's virgin desires, and setting every hormone in his young body on fire. His dick stiffened to an erection.

"Oh, my God. It is you. Hi, Party."

"Hi."

"Oh, my God."

Camille gave Party a hug. In the moment, Party inhaled her perfume deep into his lungs, and allowed himself to be hugged. The softness of Camille's chest on his shoulder and upper arm was electric.

"T–T–Told'ju."

"Stutter Man, what I tell you about standin' so fuckin' close to me like that?"

Stutter Man took a generous step back, and winked his left eye at Party, only to get caught mid-wink by Camille.

"See, now, didn't you just get poked in ya eye last week, for actin' like a damn pervert? Why you in here anyway? Monica told'ju not to come in here for a week. Make me call her."

Instead of responding, Stutter Man smirked and flipped up his eye patch, revealing a bloodshot, right eye. When Party and Camille both got a good stare at it, Stutter Man grinned from ear to ear, then flipped the eye patch back over his bruised eye. His smile was bright.

"With them big ass fuckin' veneers. Get 'em shaved down! I keep tellin' you they don't look right, Stutter Man. Party, don't his teeth look like a row of bathroom urinals?"

For ten minutes, Party listened as Camille and Stutter Man went back and forth about his teeth. Party was enjoying their company, and privately, was sensing that there was a mutual attraction going on, between him and Camille. Camille reminded him of Blac Chyna. Her body was curvy and thick, and she had a pretty face. When his cell phone started ringing, Party fished it out of his pocket, accepted the call, then placed the cell phone to his ear.

"What's up, Sab?"

"You sound like you in a good mood. Where you at?"

"The shop."

"Good, 'cause, I got some rap for you. Find some privacy."

"Alright."

From the serious tone of his brother's voice, Party immediately knew that something was wrong. As he rose from the video game, Party cracked a smile and switched his cell phone to his opposite ear when Stutter Man began doing the 'Cat Daddy' dance. Camille rolled her eyes at Stutter Man in annoyance. Believing that Camille and Stutter Man would follow him into the hair salon, Party decided to go outside to his truck.

"Where you goin', Party? See, Stutter Man . . . you irkin' him with the dumb stuff."

"Naw, he cool," Party clarified, while walking up to the front door of the barber shop. Looking over his shoulder, he held Camille's stare for a meaningful moment. "I'll be right back. This my brother. Plus, I gotta get somethin' outta my truck."

"Alright, 'cause, I can't do his pervert ass too long. Irkin'."

"Y–Y–You–You–You ir-irkin'."

"Spell it wit'out stutterin'!"

Seconds later, out in his Range Rover, Party pulled off his scully and sat it in his lap. After a quick glance back into the barber shop, Party checked his rearview mirror. Only until he saw that things behind him appeared safe, did he let himself relax.

"Look, they supposed to be doin' a shakedown today, so I'ma have to flush this phone, after we done this conversation."

"You gon' be able to get another one, right?"

"Yeah, I got a guard in here on deck. Breen know the drill."

"Oh, alright."

"So, what'chu think about the shop? You like it, right?"

"Sab, this jawn decent. Yeah, I like it. Got my name up there."

"Party, somebody that work in there fuck wit' Mommy."

The revelation caused every good feeling Party had about his barber shop to explode into pieces. He looked as several cars and SUVs began to pull up and park on both sides of the street. There were six vehicles in total. Party was suddenly feeling nervous again, and from what Sab had just told him, he knew that he had every reason to be.

"Me and Breen been tryna find out–Oh, shit. Yo, Party, the guards hittin' the block. I gotta go."

After his brother ended their call, Party leaned back and let out a sigh. His eyes stayed on the cars that had just arrived. In the backseat, he had two guns wrapped inside of a small towel, hidden inside of a gutted-basketball. There was also the contentment of knowing that his SUV was bulletproof. He discreetly began to scrutinize the drivers of each vehicle, as they exited them, and started walking over to his barber shop. He quickly assumed that they were his employees. There was a snake amongst them, or, perhaps, he had already been in contact with that person, before Sab had even called. Party shot a quick glance into his barber shop at Camille and Stutter Man. With distrust now in his heart, Party sat up and lowered his window as a pretty woman from the crowd came walking up to his truck offering him her cell phone, and a bright smile.

"You Party, right?"

Party nodded his head as he accepted the cell phone. He blinked as the cold air whipped around his face, and shot into his SUV.

"That's Breen. I'm Ashley, by the way. I'll be in the salon when you done."

"Alright."

Party placed the cell phone to his ear as he raised his window. His eyes followed the pretty female as she rejoined the rest of his employees and filed into his barber shop. For a moment, Party stared hungrily at Ashley's ass. When she looked over the shoulder of her waist-length, lynx fur, and caught him, Party shyly looked away. Had he not looked away, he would have saw the promising and bright smile that Ashley's face had produced for him.

"What's up, Breen?"

"Did Sab call you? My phone was on the charger when he called."

"I just got off the phone with him. The guards shakin' his block down. He gon' need a new phone."

"Alright."

"Breen, why you ain't tell me somebody in the shop messin' wit' my mom?"

"That's why I was stoppin' by there this afternoon."

"So, who is it?"

"We still don't know, yet."

"Who the one that handed me this phone?"

"That was Ashley."

"She the one that manage the salon, right?"

"Yeah, but, her cousin, Camille, help her a lot."

Party looked into his barber shop. Ashley and Camille were standing away from everyone else, talking privately. They appeared to be very close.

"It ain't them, is it?"

"Party, I honestly can't tell you. It could be anybody."

Snakes.

"Don't underestimate nobody, Party. Not even Stutter Man."

"So, how you find out she got somebody in there?"

"One day, I was there to collect the rent. It was real busy, so I called myself helpin' out, by answerin' the phone. At first, I ain't know who it was. After some back and forth, with me askin' who she wanted to speak to, and did she have an appointment, or somethin' along those lines, she just started laughin'. We both know how creepy her laugh is, right? So, now, I'm lookin' at the phone, like, it can't be. Then, she just started talkin' to me in her regular voice. Party, I almost lost my fuckin' mind in there. Like, literally.

The crazy bitch told me she got eyes everywhere, then hung up."

"So, she in Philly, then?"

"Not necessarily. The number she called from was blocked. She could still be anywhere."

"I wonder which one of them it is."

"We'll figure it out. In the meantime, act normal. There is some good news, though. Remember Manny Yunk and Nacky?"

"My dad friends?"

"Party, that's their neighborhood. Don't shit happen around there, without them knowin' it. They know you back, Party."

Party stared into his barber shop again. All of his employees were staring back out at him; even Stutter Man. Their faces appeared innocent, and Party wanted to believe it was maybe just the excitement of him being there, but with all that he now was aware of, it was naturally easy for him to rule that out.

"Party, trust me, I wanted to fire everybody. Me and Sab had a long talk about it. Sab think the person can lead us to y'all mom."

"And I guess, I'm the damn bait, huh?"

"Unfortunately, Party. It'll all work out. I'll be by there later, okay?"

"Alright, Breen."

While putting on his hat, Party twisted and looked into the backseat at his basketball, considering removing the guns from it, and placing them both on his waist. The idea became distracted by Ashley's cell phone. Someone was making an attempt to facetime with her.

Distractions.

Party climbed out of his truck, palming Ashley's cell phone and his own. The anxiety of meeting the rest of his employees had put knots in his stomach. He was upset with his older brother and sister-in-law, because he would have preferred to know that his mother had secret ties with one of his employees, before showing up. He hadn't had time to prepare for it mentally, and this is what bothered Party most. As Party neared the front door of his barber shop, his attention was pulled to a black, mini-van, as it came racing down Marshall Street.

Something.

Wrong.

The black, mini-van, came to a screeching stop directly beside Party's Range Rover. More out of curiosity, than fear, Party turned and faced the street. When the side-door of the mini-van was suddenly snatched open, and three masked men, with assault rifles came rushing out, with their eyes on him, Party took in a deep breath and held it. His mother had won again.

Chapter Three

It was February 11th, 2013. Above the dark wilderness of Poconos, Pennsylvania, the midnight sky was dropping a steady shower of snow. So far, eleven inches had fallen. According to local weather reports, a total of nineteen inches of snow was predicted to fall in the mountains, before the next morning arrived. Temperatures had dropped below the minus level, and the air was cold and crisp.

Rock 'n Roll Rhonda, as she was notoriously known, was standing ankle-deep in a pile of snow, holding her cell phone up to her ear, and soaking in the beautiful scene all around her. She was at the edge of a snow-covered pier, that jutted out twenty-five feet over a frozen lake. The entire lake was blanketed with snow. In the background of the quiet wilderness, the mountains and tall trees were also wearing layers of fresh snow. Being alone, and exposed to the frigid temperatures wasn't bothering Rock 'n Roll Rhonda one bit. At the moment, her emotions and thoughts were elsewhere.

"So, I'm only guessin', but is it safe for me to assume that chu still not ready to come back to Philly?"

"Nope."

"Rhonda, it's been a month."

Rock 'n Roll Rhonda rolled her eyes at her cousin's comment, as she opened her mouth and stuck out her tongue to catch a falling snowflake. While the tiny piece of snow was dissolving in her mouth, she entertained the idea of rudely ending the phone call, so she could return back to her own private thinking, but she decided against it a moment later.

"You never told me this was part of your plan, before you got out, Rhonda."

"It's a lot that wasn't a part of my plan, Zay," Rock 'n Roll Rhonda clarified, before switching her cell phone to her opposite ear. Her sudden movement had caused the deer and fawn she had been watching, to both pause in their tracks, and return her stare, as the pair crossed over the frozen lake, over sixty feet away from where she stood. "What happened to Tia wasn't. Goin' back to jail wasn't. Us goin' to war with Splash wasn't. Zay, what happened to Uncle Tuna and Brittany wasn't, either. Nothin' in my life has ever been a part of my fuckin' plan, Zay. Was what happened to Bayyinah a part of yours? No. Zay, my daughter would be turnin' two tomorrow. We both know why she not, though, right?"

"You made a mistake, Rhonda."

"Exactly. One of the biggest ones of my fuckin' life. A mistake that wasn't a part of my plan."

"Alright . . . okay."

"Zay, I just want some time to myself. Please."

"Okay."

"You'll be the first person I call when I'm ready to come home. While I'm away, just keep an eye on Liberty for me."

"Why? What don't I know?"

"Well, you already know I let her stay at my condo. I can't put my finger on it, but she's up to somethin', Zay."

"Do it involve Victoria Beauvais?"

"It could. That's just the thing . . . she don't know I can go to this app on my phone and listen to anything she says in my apartment, or does, but I'm tryna respect her privacy, Zay. She just be actin' real weird whenever I call her."

"I'll see what I can find out. I'm sorry for disturbin' your peace, and I'm always a call away, alright? I love you."

"Love you, too. As Salaamu Alaykum."

"Wa Laykum As Salaam Wa Rahmatullah."

A day after her release from a Philadelphia county prison, Rock 'n Roll Rhonda had packed several suitcases, and without telling anyone, she left Philadelphia in the late hours of the night. A private limousine service had chauffeured her out to the Poconos mountains, where her deceased cousin owned a timeshare cabin. Rock 'n Roll Rhonda had planned the secret vacation, long before her release. Two weeks had gone by, before she had felt inclined to power her cell phone on, and inform anyone of her whereabouts. Zainab, her older cousin, had been extremely upset with her, because she had initially jumped to conclusions, and had feared the worst had happened to her cousin.

Rock 'n Roll Rhonda wanted to be alone, and time to mourn the lives of all the people she had recently lost. She was feeling depressed and emotionally fatigued. After watching the deer and fawn disappear into the line of snow-covered trees, on the far end of the frozen lake, Rock 'n Roll Rhonda turned around and started walking down the snow-covered pier. She took three steps, before she made an abrupt stop.

Savages.

In the Poconos mountains, the conflict between predator and prey was normally a tension present amongst the wildlife. People often sought out the atmosphere of the cold mountains, for its tranquility, and not to find any trouble. That had been Rock 'n Roll Rhonda's intentions. As Rock 'n Roll Rhonda watched the dark SUV come to a sudden stop, causing the one trailing it to do the same, she wanted to believe the two vehicles had mistakenly made a turn onto the wrong property. She gave them a moment, considering that once they quickly recognized their error, both SUVs would be reversing and going on their way in the correct direction.

Before her death, Rock 'n Roll Rhonda's aunt, Quintessa Bancroft, had shared the cabin with an old, Israeli couple, who resided in Rochester, New York. The wife was an Investment banker, and the husband was an International arms dealer. The rich couple had felt indebted to Rock 'n Roll Rhonda's aunt, because while she had been going over plans to redesign their home, back in 1999, she had witnessed the murder of one of their house staff, and had kept quiet about the incident. For her obvious display of loyalty, the Israeli couple had made Rock 'n Roll Rhonda's aunt a partner in all of their commercial properties, and also chose to share their cabin in the Poconos mountains with her as well.

One sight of the bi-level cabin would inspire romance in anyone. On the inside, a person could easily forget they were surrounded by a massive wilderness. The cabin was stuffed with two bedrooms, three and a half baths, a spa, and a game room. Behind the handsome cabin, the landscapers had placed a swimming pool in a clearing in the woods. Of course, this amenity could only be enjoyed during the summer. As for any fans of the winter, there were six snow mobiles and a bunch of ski equipment inside of a small barn, sitting off to the left of the long, gravel driveway. The closest house to the cabin, was an even nicer cabin, located on the opposite side of Locust Lake, owned by a female Supreme Court judge.

The driveway that led up to the cabin was a quarter of a mile in distance, and after a few turns, there was a straight-away that climbed with the snowy terrain. The driveway branched off from a road that ran to and from a main highway, and a nearby ski resort. The driveway was outlined with a stretch of tall trees, and it took about five to ten minutes of driving, before the cabin, Locust Lake, and the rest of the surrounding property became visible. This unobstructed view was provided by two large clearings on both sides of the driveway. In the summer, these portions of land were giant beds of grass.

Rock 'n Roll Rhonda stared down across the sea of snow at the two dark SUVs, becoming more impatient as time went by. She was sure the occupants of both vehicles saw her. She wondered if the sight of her had caused them to stop, and if so, and they were heading to the right destination, how did they know she was there. Only her two cousins knew she was at the cabin. Until now, Rock 'n Roll Rhonda hadn't thought about the two guns she had packed in one of her suitcases.

"Okay," Rock 'n Roll Rhonda exhaled, walking again, and also noticing out of the corner of her left eye that her movement had seemingly provoked the dark SUVs to do the same. Because they were proceeding ahead, this forced her to identify her new company as threats. "Zay wouldn't even think about doin' some shit like this to me. She fear Allah too much. Zay love me enough not to. It was Liberty. She did this."

Rock 'n Roll Rhonda started running. Stumbling twice, and falling down to her knees once, she had managed to get her cell phone out of her pocket. In some places, the snow came up to her knees, making her race for the cabin a difficult one. Still, she ran relentlessly, because she knew without a shadow of a doubt, if she wanted to stay alive, she had to get to her guns. The two SUVs had quickened their own pace. Rock 'n Roll Rhonda could hear her heartbeat drumming in her ears, as she pressed her cell phone against her ear, while looking over her shoulder to see how far the trucks were. When she heard her cousin's voice in her left ear, tears came to her eyes. In that same moment, she heard the unmistakable crack of a gunshot. As she turned to look over her shoulder, a hot bullet slammed into the back of her right thigh, sending her falling face-first into the snow.

"Rhonda?"

"Zay, they–They about to kill me. It was Liberty."

Chapter Four

Scandalous.

"Liberty, I just need to be able to trust you. If you show me I can count on you, I'll give you whatever you fuckin' want. Anything."

"Marry me."

"What?"

"Come home and marry me, "Liberty insisted, before switching her cell phone to her opposite ear, while parking her cousin's car. Once she was satisfied with her parking, she killed the engine, let out a sigh, then resumed talking into her cell phone. "Look, until me, what other chick you had out here, that'chu could really rely on, Splash? Excludin' ya aunt? She don't count. And we both know how fuckin' complicated ya goals are. You been tryna get'cha son back. You tryna come home. Thanks to me, Rhonda not even a problem for you no more. That bitch gone with the fuckin' wind."

"Since when?"

"Last night."

"Get the fuck outta here. How?"

"I got him," Liberty mouthed, looking over to the passenger seat at her best friend, Storm. The smile of admiration on her best friend's face added to her confidence, as she reached into the backseat, grabbed her pocketbook, and prepared to step out of the car to the cold, morning weather. "When I come visit you this afternoon, I'll give you all the details about Rhonda. In the meantime, give some thought to what I asked you."

"About marryin' you? You was serious?"

Liberty Madeline Shafesky was a beautiful, and tough-spirited, 25-year-old, who absolutely hated when anyone thought less than what she thought of herself. She was conniving most of the time, and bi-sexual whenever she felt like it. Growing up, she had convinced herself that the world owed her. This was partially her father's fault, because before his death, Liberty had gotten anything she had asked for. She had never been refused of anything. The death of her father had been a cold slap to the face for Liberty. The one year anniversary of her father's murder was approaching, and as it did, Liberty was becoming more and more impulsive with her actions to find her father's killer, and to be successful at carving out her own space as a wife, a mother, and a woman with wealth.

As a child, before the growth of her judgmental personality, and sharp tongue, she had dealt quietly with a lot of finger-pointing, snide remarks, and insensitive comments. In some instances, the adults had been worse than the children. Liberty's father had been a black man with skin the color of the darkest night, and her mother was a full-blooded, Irish woman. The blend of their DNA had produced an odd, but strikingly, beautiful child.

Liberty had her father's complexion, her mother's silky red hair, and a set of eyes that had only been gifted to her great-grandmother back in Ireland. Liberty's left eye was blue, and her right eye was green. As young as 6-years-old, her mother had begun dyeing her hair black, and had forced her to wear a green, eye contact lens, to hide her one blue eye. During each and every last one of these physical transformations, Liberty had gone through the emotional wreckage of feeling ugly in her mother's eyes. Her father had overcompensated by spoiling her with the gifts he believed any girl her age would want. By her teenage years, the Barbie dolls, bicycles, and amusement parks, had matured into designer clothes, credit cards, and trips, to wherever she wanted to go.

At only 5'4" tall, Liberty was a lot of woman. Her outlook on life, and way of thinking, was as unique as her look. She could easily be a successful business owner, or make lots of money as a stripper, tantalizing men with her curvaceous body. She had over a hundred thousand followers on social media, and all of her ex-boyfriends were still following her pages, in hopes of one day reclaiming her attention and heart. Liberty was only attracted to elite men. Her standards were high, and her expectations were even higher.

Liberty no longer disguised her hair's natural color, or wore contact lenses. With the fashion industry becoming so daring, it had given Liberty the freedom she had always wanted. She had piercings in both of her nipples, and one in her clit that glowed in the dark. Liberty was a borderline nympho, and one of her biggest goals in life, was to one day outdo her deceased cousin, Tia, who, up until her death, had always been viewed as their family's proudest success story.

Matriarchs.

Liberty was two months into the new year, and was still clinging stubbornly to her New Year's resolutions. Finding Victoria Beauvais, the woman responsible for her father's murder, was at the very top of her list. It was a vow she had unsuccessfully left 2012 with. There was also her determination of becoming a part owner of the popular, Philadelphia nightclub, Gossip Alley. This was a private goal of Liberty's, just as the hopes of her one day marrying the nightclub's incarcerated owner had been, up until a few moments ago.

"Splash, let's back up," Liberty suggested, as she glanced up at the rearview mirror, then at the driver's side mirror. She was allowing herself to fall behind schedule, and this was causing her tolerance to run low. "I came to you. When I made that decision to come up there to see you, and I poured my fuckin' heart out to you, I was jeapordizin' my own life that day. It wasn't shit you could've done to protect me from in there, Splash. Tia dead. Sabia down at that fuckin' federal buildin' downtown with half a fuckin' body. My dad dead. I'm all you got, Splash. I've given you more than enough reasons to trust me. Haven't I? If this shit blow up in our faces, I'll be left standin' with more to lose, than you."

"And that's exactly why my concern of ya loyalty is to the level that it is, Liberty. Ya goals ain't because you love me. Liberty, you love you."

"So, my love under a microscope?" Liberty asked, shaking her head in disbelief. Her feelings were hurt. "But that makes sense, Splash. You so lovin', right? Boy, bye. And loyal, too, right? Why Tia ain't know you was still in touch with Sabia? You sent that Haitian guy to kill Zay. You made him kill Brittany. For what? Kyzer told Rhonda that you was gon' set Sabia up for him. Splash, you love you, just like I love me. I gotta go. Bye."

Upset, Liberty stepped out of her cousin's silver Lincoln, and took a moment to adjust the strap of her tote bag over left shoulder. While doing the same, Storm gave her a questioning look over the roof of the car.

"Bitch, don't start. My father, her fuckin' son."

"Lib, think this shit through. Her sons probably hate her as much as you do. Lib, she killed their dad, too. We can work with them, Lib. It's not too late, yet."

"Storm, you can stay in the car, or come with me. Make up ya fuckin' mind."

Storm sighed and followed Liberty across 9th Street, and joined her on the sidewalk. There, Liberty gave Storm a questioning look of her own, before beginning to walk. Both of them were dressed in the traditional over garments Muslim women wore. Nothing was visible on them, but their eyes. Above them, the Wednesday morning sky was gray and spotted with lots of clouds. The clouds were being ushered east by some viciously, cold winds. As Liberty and Storm walked east on Dauphin Street, the black material on the lower-half of their over garments swayed in the wind behind them. When they reached the corner of 8th and Dauphin, all four doors on a parked, Jeep Cherokee, down at the corner of Franklin and Dauphin came open, and four women dressed exactly like Liberty and Storm climbed out. No looks were exchanged, or words were spoken. After the four women joined Liberty and Storm, together, with Liberty in the lead, the six women crossed Dauphin Street, and began walking north up 8th street.

Omens.

9:14 a.m.

"Somethin' ain't right, bro. She said nine exactly. It's almost—"

"Yo, this them right here, Murf. Go make sure he ready. Yo, don't start whoppin', 'til they all inside this mu'fucker."

Party overheard the conversation between Khalid and Murf, and immediately started to sweat. His heart began slamming against his chest like it desperately wanted to escape it. His abduction had now come to the fateful moment when he would finally get to meet the person responsible for his kidnapping. Party exhaled a nervous breath, as Murf came rushing around one of the tall stacks of boxes with his gun down by his side.

"They here. You ready?"

Nervously, Party swallowed and nodded his head. His eyes left Murf and went to the direction of the new voices he could hear coming into the dimly lit, building, where he had been held captive for the last 24 hours. The building was once a popular nightclub in North Philadelphia, and was located on 8th and Dauphin, across from an old factory. It now housed hundreds and hundreds of boxes, packed with kitchen, and dinette furniture, and bedroom sets. The new owner had plans of turning the property into a furniture store in the spring. Some of the boxes in the building were stacked as high as the ceiling. The moving company had placed the boxes in aisles in some parts of the building, and in others, the boxes were just stacked up against the walls, or as high as the movers could get them, without the potential threat of the boxes toppling over. In some places, there were openings and gaps, and Party had been smuggled into the building, then ushered to a metal chair in one of these areas the prior evening, and left alone. The men had tied Party's lower legs to the chair with socks, and had handcuffed his arms behind his back, and hadn't bothered to remove the dark pillowcase from his head, before they all had departed the cold and silent building.

In 2-hour-intervals, different men had come and gone. Party had been allowed to use the bathroom, and was once handfed a fast food sandwich, and given a few drinks of some bottled water. Each time, the men had come in groups of twos, and had kept their ski masks on.

By dawn, Party felt enraged and he began experiencing an unforgivable string of mood swings. There were minute-long bouts, where dark moments of depression had defeated him to crying uncontrollably. There were moments, where the burden of his regrets in life had gotten so heavy for his shoulders, it had left him deeply conscious of God for almost an hour. He had moments, where he pitied himself. He wondered how his older brother would respond to the news of his death, and if his uncle would finally make it his personal duty of tracking down his mother for once. Anger was the mood that prevailed the longest with Party. The flame of this dangerous emotion in him had burned violently, reducing every thought of his mother to ashes, and had caused all of his final wishes to be that she soon met a merciless retaliation.

Until now, Party had never wanted to come within mere inches of his mother. Until now, Party had never possessed the conviction that he could see his mother, and want to take her life with his own hands.

Until.

Now.

At exactly 6:49 a.m., Party had met the leader of the men who had kidnapped him. The young man, had personally removed the pillowcase from Party's head, and had uncuffed him as well. He had also returned two cell phones to Party; one that belonged to Party, and the one Party had never gotten the chance to give back to Ashley.

The group of men who had kidnapped Party were all members of a violent, North Philadelphia gang, dubbed, 'The Kidnap Kids.' The Kidnap Kids worked in silence, and while existence of their group was known by Philadelphia police, and even the mayor, their personal identities were only known by their members. They moved independently, and were led and operated by Khalid. Khalid was tall, dark, and in his twenties, and no one to be underestimated, or played with. He was from 12th and Susquehanna, but gossip of his refined expertise in the kidnapping business had gotten his group jobs all over the country.

Until Party, Khalid had never once entertained the idea of negotiating the price of freedom with anyone he had been hired to kidnap. It was unthought of. The act itself would violate the trust held between The Kidnap Kids, and the person, or people, who had sought out their services. Khalid hadn't been physically involved with any of The Kidnap Kids' jobs, since his first two. He normally let Murf run their outside movements, and stayed behind the scenes. Last night, all that had changed. In the late hours of the night, the underworld in Philadelphia had erupted into a gossiping frenzy, after an anonymous subscriber on Snap-Chat had uploaded a shocking video for all to see. The seconds-long video had shown a young woman running, before being shot, somewhere in the wilderness, where it had been snowing heavily. Several minutes later, a second video showed the woman being kicked, punched, and violently dragged up the steps of a cabin by two masked men. The third, and final video, had shown the woman's bruised face, before she had spit into the direction of the person recording her, as they laughed at her.

The post for all three videos had read, 'Rock & Roll . . . RIP.' All three videos had reached over two hundred thousand views, and the numbers were still steadily climbing.

Khalid had viewed all three videos, and had drawn one conclusion. The person who had hired him had claimed to be Rock 'n Roll Rhonda, but during a secret meeting of theirs, as he and Murf were departing, Rock 'n Roll Rhonda, or any of the Muslim women with her, seemed to not know how to respond to his Islamic greetings correctly. While walking to their cars, the uncomfortable moment had caused Khalid and Murf to eye one another strangely. In Philadelphia, Rock 'n Roll Rhonda's reputation preceded her. Khalid and Murf had both felt honored to be working with her. They had shared a common enemy once. After their meeting, however, Khalid had shared with Murf that something about Rock 'n Roll Rhonda had been off, and it had nothing to do with him never hearing that she had blue eyes.

Upon witnessing the viral videos, Khalid had been convinced that the woman in them was the real Rock 'n Roll Rhonda, and that the blue-eyed woman, coming to meet him the next morning to kill Party, was an imposter.

She and her friends had dressed like Muslim women to disguise themselves. It was this blatant disrespect to his religion, that had disgusted Khalid, and had inspired him to go and introduce himself to Party. As the sun rose, so had a new plot.

Traps.

9:16 a.m.

"Ya father didn't get this chance."

Party nodded his head as Murf replaced the dark pillowcase over his head, and hurriedly backed away from him. With his vision now obstructed, his hearing grew more keen. He could hear Khalid closing the door to the building, then locking it. Him hearing Murf cock the hammers on both of his guns, as the sound of approaching footsteps became louder, made him shut his eyes and search for the level of concentration he would need, if he expected to outlive the mystery woman, who was coming to take his life. His father wasn't given this chance.

Rock.

"The element of surprise only lasts but so long," Party remembered, thinking of some tactical advice his uncle had once shared with him, during one of their Saturday morning jogs. Picturing in his mind what his eyes had shown him last, before Murf had placed the pillowcase over his head, he took in a deep breath through his nostrils, and as he slowly lowered his head, he exhaled out of his mouth. "Murf is on my right. I need to put some distance between us. They gotta turn that aisle and come on a angle, to my left. Khalid gon' either stay out in the aisle, and shoot from there, or he gon' come all the way around, so he'll be out of me 'n Murf's line of fire. None of us got silencers. I gotta make it to that back door, and—"

"Take that thing off his head."

&.

Roll.

47

Party went into action the moment the pillowcase was removed from his head, and he was able to see again. His uncle had taught him well, and had prepared him for life threatening moments like this, and far worse. Using the balls of both feet, Party pushed off the floor, sending the wooden chair he was sitting on backwards to its hind legs. All six women paused at Party's reaction, believing fear had caused this type of response from him. The distraction gave Murf the moment he needed to raise his guns. Before Murf was able to decide who he would shoot at first, in one swift motion, Party removed his hands from behind his back, and joined them together. He aimed his brother's automatic shotgun at the woman standing directly in front of him, and squeezed the trigger, before falling back to the floor.

The shotgun blast was deafening, and the damage it caused was intimidating. Its impact had lifted the woman from her feet, and had sent her body flying into the women behind her.

Before any of the women could react, Murf began shooting at them, striking one in the head twice, and hitting another several times in her upper back. He moved to his left as Party rolled to his knees, and started crawling in the direction of the aisle, leading to the rear of the building, where Party would find the unlocked door that would provide his escape.

Murf continued shooting, and was joined by Khalid, who had found a vantage point on top of a stack of boxes in a far-off corner of the building. After Khalid was certain that Party was out of the building, and had gotten away safely, he shot his gun several more times, then retraced his steps back down to the floor and shouted for Murf to follow him.

The interior of the building sounded like it was imploding, as echoes of the gunshots consumed its space.

Sounds of the violent symphony had reached the classrooms and hallways of a nearby school.

Liberty, Storm, and their friend, Nasha, were the only three left alive from their group. Their bodies were motionless down on the floor, in a pile, as the blood of their dead friends was slowly pooling around them. Liberty squeezed Storm's hand tightly when Murf shot in their direction, before taking off into a sprint and disappearing down one of the aisles. Had he watched them a moment longer, Murf would have realized that only some of the women were dead, and that three of them were simply just pretending.

Mistakes.

Chapter Five

The night before . . .
1:43 a.m.

At the dark SUV, Zainab paused for a quick look inside. She readjusted her gloved hands around the handle of her Glock 40, ready to aim and shoot at anyone she saw. As Zainab cautiously looked into the back windows of the SUV, then slowly moved forward to the driver's side door, her group of friends kept their eyes on the cabin up ahead. The heavy snowfall was causing poor visibility, but Zainab viewed this element as an advantage.

Zainab was a Muslim woman with few weak areas in her heart. Her love and faith in God had instilled a level of discipline in her soul that most men would never reach. At night, she stood up and prayed, while others slept. Paradise was her goal, and she worked extremely hard for it. Zainab's friends valued her advice, her company, and they all thought highly of her. Due to this, even the husbands of her closest friends had insisted that they be allowed to join the rescue party, who hoped to save Rock 'n Roll Rhonda from her captors. They knew just how much Zainab's younger cousin meant to her. The group traveled to the Poconos in three vehicles; Zainab's BMW, a Chevy Suburban, and a Nissan Titan. Everyone was dressed in white, as an effort to camouflage with the snow. There were eleven of them.

Madness.

The slap was vicious, and swung hard, and its impact sent Rock 'n Roll Rhonda down to the floor. Blood spilled from her mouth as she barely managed to bring herself up to her hands and knees. She knew that her death was imminent, and that she had yet to see the worst of her suffering. Through swollen eyes, she looked across the living area of the cabin, and stared into the eyes of Yasmeen Bey. She saw satisfaction in the deaf woman's eyes. Forcing a grin on her bruised face, she slowly raised her right hand and flipped up her middle finger. Without warning, the masked man to her left gave her a violent kick to the side of her face, as the masked man behind her, and the one to her right, both tucked their guns into the waistbands of their jeans, and took off their coats. She felt too weak to fight back, or to put up any kind of defense.

"Where you at, Zay?" Rock 'n Roll Rhonda wondered, thinking about her cousin, as the three men began to rip and tear her clothes from her body. Tears of anger and humiliation escaped her eyes, as she fought with desperation to keep her bra and panties on. "Allah, not– Please, not like this. No. Not like this. Allah, if you let them rape me, my body will be impure when I die."

Rock 'n Roll Rhonda was no match for the three men. She let out a shrill cry when one of them dug a finger into the bullet wound on the back of her right thigh. The pain was excruciating, and was almost enough to bring her to the point of begging for death. As she groaned in pain, and her body twisted in agony, one of the masked men dropped a hard knee on the center of her back to keep her still. Unable to move, Rock 'n Roll Rhonda screamed at the top of her lungs as one of the men spread her ass cheeks, while another roughly jammed the barrel of his gun into her anus.

It intrigued Yasmeen Bey to see Rock 'n Roll Rhonda rendered to such a defeated position, and so vulnerable. She couldn't stop herself from smiling. She wished her deaf ears could hear the authentic agony in Rock 'n Roll Rhonda's screams. She had been waiting for this moment for so long, it almost seemed to good to be true.

Yasmeen Bey was born and raised in South Philadelphia, but she owned a beautiful mansion in Patterson, New Jersey, where she shared her estate with her daughter-in-law, and two grandchildren. She was born deaf, and viewed the world through inquisitive, brown eyes. She was a faithful Muslim, and on a daily basis, she wore a face veil, and black, over garments, to cover her body. At fifty-years-old, she was a successful, businesswoman, who owned over two dozen daycare centers, stretching from South Boston, down to Orlando, Florida. Yasmeen Bey wasn't someone to make enemies with, and she knew how to hold a grudge. Three years earlier, Rock 'n Roll Rhonda had kidnapped her, because her son had kidnapped Rock 'n Roll Rhonda's cousin.

Night.

Of.

Redemption.

The three men paused and gave Yasmeen Bey a questioning look when Rock 'n Roll Rhonda lost consciousness, and her body went limp on the floor. An eerie silence swept through the cabin. The three men were exhausted. They had been fighting and torturing Rock 'n Roll Rhonda for hours. Yasmeen Bey gave all three men a look of disgust as she rose from the couch. She said something in sign language with her hands as she walked around the coffee table. Her eyes were angry and fixed on Rock 'n Roll Rhonda's motionless body as she removed her gun from her pocketbook. The three men eyed her cautiously.

Outside, Zainab had just made it safely to the porch of the cabin as a dark SUV had pulled onto the property, and was driving up the pathway to the cabin. This immediately caused everyone with Zainab to focus on the approaching SUV. Inside of the cabin, Yasmeen Bey was only two steps away from Rock 'n Roll Rhonda, and a moment from killing her execution style, when her cell phone began to buzz in the right pocket of her fur vest. Yasmeen Bey pulled out her cell phone and stared at the new text message sent by her daughter-in-law, and with one breath, she suddenly turned to the door of the cabin, and started running towards it, shooting at it wildly.

War.

Zainab didn't budge or flinch when the hot bullets came splintering through the cabin's door. The sense of urgency she felt in rescuing her younger cousin had removed all concerns she might have ordinarily felt for her own safety. She would prefer to meet death, than to fail her younger cousin. Behind her, Rock 'n Roll Rhonda's blood was stained across the snow. Once the gunshots ceased in the cabin, Zainab dropped down to one knee, aimed her Glock at the door with both hands, shot ten times, then she rolled across the porch to her left, so her friends, Taheerah, Maryam, and Fatimah, could finish what she had started. As Zainab hopped off the porch, and went running around to the rear of the cabin, Taheerah, Maryam, and Fatimah, unleashed a wave of bullets at the cabin's front door. All three women were cradling assault rifles.

The silence of the night no longer existed. As the snow continued to fall, and the violent noise of so many guns being fired shattered the cold air, the property that the cabin sat on looked like it had been ripped from the pages of an old civil war book.

Yasmeen Bey's daughter-in-law, and three Muslim women, had exited the dark SUV with handguns, and an assault rifle, and they quickly began spraying bullets at anyone dressed in white. This sent Zainab's friends diving into the snow, and running for cover as all of them returned fire from any angle that they could. Everyone on the scene had recognized that they all shared the same religion, and this fact had crept into the moral fabrics of all of their souls, but not one of them dared to stop trading bullets.

Zainab knew the cabin well. She had been coming out to the cabin, since she had been a teenager. She knew every deep area of the lake, and the places where it was most shallow. Zainab knew all of the trails, and without help, she also knew which trees produced poisonous leaves and berries. Her cousin, Tia, had taught her everything she had needed to know about the cabin, and its surroundings. At the rear of the cabin, Zainab hurried over to a window that provided a view into the cabin's kitchen. Before Zainab could steal a glance inside, the cabin's rear door was pulled open. Zainab aimed her gun at the man who came rushing out, and shot him twice in the face. As the masked man fell face-first down the wooden steps, Zainab stepped over his lifeless body, shooting him three more times in the back of the head. The snow beneath him, and around him, quickly became stained with the blood from his wounds.

The man Zainab had killed had been attempting to flee from her friends. Taheerah, Maryam, and Fatimah, had made it into the cabin, and after a brief exchange of gunfire, both of his friends had been shot down to the floor. Before their entrance, Yasmeen Bey had fled upstairs. She was hiding in the closet of an upstairs bedroom.

"In here, Zay! We found her! Here she go, right here!"

"Oh, my God! Taheerah, you got hit!"

Zainab felt her heart shudder in her chest at hearing Maryam's words. Her eyes were soaking in all of the visual details as she hurried through the cabin's kitchen. The cabin looked like a tornado had been through it. Paintings and pictures had been knocked off the walls. Furniture in the dining area was flipped over and tossed aside. In the living area, Zainab halted, looking from Taheerah, then, down at her cousin. The dynamics of the situation had quickly been altered, and Zainab saw the proof of this on the facial expressions of her three friends.

Taheerah let her AR-7 assault rifle, drop to the floor as Maryam and Fatimah helped her stand. Holding both hands against her stomach, Taheerah held Zainab's stare. Zainab's eyes were watery, because she knew that Taheerah was two and a half months pregnant with her first child. A stain of blood was slowly growing across her white jacket.

Remorse.

"Get her outta here!" Zainab screamed, as she dropped to the floor by her cousin's side. To find her younger cousin at a level of such vulnerability was almost paralyzing. "Fatimah, tell Najee and Raqeeb to come in here! It's time to go!"

Zainab turned her cousin gently and placed her ear to her cousin's chest. All of the shooting going on outside made it difficult for her to hear her cousin's heartbeat. Before Najee and Raqeeb arrived, she wanted to cover her cousin's naked body. She had begun to cry, without realizing it, and seeing the condition her younger cousin's body was in seemed to be draining all of the energy she had left in her heart. It took her a few minutes, but Zainab managed to put on the clothes that Rock 'n Roll Rhonda had been wearing. The gunshot wound to the back of her leg was bleeding profusely, and there was a dark stream of blood flowing from her anus. That wound was playing horrible tricks on Zainab's mind the most. She knew that if her younger cousin made it through this experience, and was to survive this ordeal, her behavior once she was able to function again on her own would be explosive and toxic.

Najee came running into the cabin first. Raqeeb was a few seconds behind him. Without speaking, they both hurried over to Rock 'n Roll Rhonda and picked her up, and quickly headed back out of the cabin. Zainab remembered who her cousin had told her was responsible for everything that was happening. On her way to the Poconos, Zainab had attempted to call her younger cousin, Liberty, several times, and each call had gone unanswered. She had even sent direct messages to her on Instagram. Zainab thought of this as she ran to each masked man and tore off his ski mask.

Zainab stood over the man she had killed behind the cabin. Removing his mask had pulled away pieces of his skull and brain matter. His face wasn't familiar either, so she ran back into the cabin. She stopped to pick up Taheerah's AR-7 assault rifle, and never looked back as she ran outside to the falling snow and flying bullets. She had the slightest clue that she had left an enemy behind.

Yasmeen Bey couldn't hear any of the shooting going on outside. She was in a fetal position on the floor of the closet, with her gun aimed at the closet's door. Everyone that had come with her to kill Rock 'n Roll Rhonda had been murdered, and she assumed this to be true. She prayed that her hiding place would go undiscovered, so she could avenge them all.

Hatred.

Chapter Six

Redeemed.

Party's barbershop was crowded and busy, as it typically was on a weekday morning. No one noticed that Party was out front, or seemed to be at all bothered by Party's abduction at the barbershop the day before. From Party's perspective, what had happened to him the prior morning was no one's concern, and things were just simply business as usual. This helped Party summon the anger and frustration he wanted to have when he confronted all of his employees.

There was a hazardous fire burning wildly inside of Party, and his mind was entertaining a lot of dangerous ideas. He was happy to be alive, but he had a lot of reasons why he was angry with the world. Party snatched open the rear, driver's side door of his truck, and leaned inside. He pulled his brother's automatic shotgun from his waist and slid it beneath his driver's seat, then he grabbed his basketball from the backseat and used his elbow to close the door.

It had taken Party thirty minutes to make it from 8th and Dauphin, down to Marshall and Girard. Above him, two police helicopters had hovered in the sky, and on more than one occasion, he had come drastically close to tossing his brother's gun, because of the heavy police presence in the area. While crossing the intersection of 6th and Diamond, an unmarked car had pulled beside him and had followed him as he was walking south on 6th street, until he had reached Berks Street. Party had struggled with the urge to run the entire time.

At eighteen, Party had a youthful appearance, and a naturally exuberant attitude. When he did become upset about something, the innocence in his brown eyes quickly vanished, and his facial expression became terrifyingly mean. The older Party got, the more he resembled his father. He stood an even 5' 8" tall, and weighed 185 pounds. Like his father, Party had a handsome face, almond brown skin, wavy hair, and a boyish smile that could dazzle the clothes off of a nun.

The laughing and talking immediately stopped when Party walked into the barber shop, and stood in the entrance with his basketball tucked beneath his left arm. He was using his right foot to keep the front door open. All four barbers stopped cutting hair and gave him an astonished stare.

"If you don't work here, get the fuck out!" Party yelled, looking specifically at all of the waiting clients, and the four men seated in the barber chairs, getting their haircuts. When no one budged, he dug a hand into his basketball and pulled out a gun, then used his other hand to remove another one. "Alright, we can do it this way! It don't matter to me! I'm Party! I own this fuckin' shop! If you not one of my fuckin' barbers, get the fuck out!!"

Party used his thumbs to cock the hammers on his twin, 357 Ruger revolvers. His angry eyes started looking for a challenge as he took a threatening step forward, and looked at the face of every man, sitting or standing. When he let his basketball drop to the floor, people started moving for the door.

"Fair warnin'!" Party warned, while walking by each barber's station, heading for the hair salon. Out of his peripheral vision, he saw the barber at the third station giving him a dirty look as he disrespectfully continued to finish cutting his client's hair. "If anybody other than my barbers still in here when I come back, what happen to you, is ya fault . . . not mine."

Party and Camille collided in the small hallway, leading to the hair salon. Camille was shocked, and couldn't believe her eyes.

"Party?"

Party snatched his arm away when Camille reached out to touch him, as he walked around her dismissively. Her beauty no longer impressed Party. He finished stuffing his guns down into the front pockets of his jeans, and with Camille following closely behind him, he pushed the hair salon's pink door open and stormed inside.

"Party, who you lookin' for?"

Party ignored Camille as he stared around the empty hair salon. He could feel her eyes all over him. Her perfume had the smell of bubblegum.

"Are you okay? How you get away?"

Party spun around and grabbed Camille by the throat, then backed her into a wall. She made no effort to free herself. Glaring into Camille's frightened eyes, Party pulled a gun from his pocket and put the chrome barrel under Camille's chin. A teardrop crept out of Camille's left eye.

"Stop actin' like you really give a fuck about what happened to me yesterday!"

"Party, I–"

"You on my mom side?!"

"What? Party, no! I–I never even met her. I swear."

Party tightened his grip around Camille's neck as he searched her watery eyes for untruths. He only saw fear and confusion, so he released her and slowly backed away.

Camille's eyes went from Party's, down to the gun in his hand, then to the handle of his other gun, poking out of his pocket.

"You here to kill somebody?"

"Anybody that's on my mom team," Party warned, leaving the hair salon. He removed his other gun from his pocket, as he headed back to his barber shop, with Camille right behind him. "It don't matter who, either. I ain't gon' be in here, worryin' about who I got around me. Oh, nigga, you thought I was playin'?"

Party handed Camille his guns. The barbers at the first, second, and fourth barber's station, all hurried off the barber's stage. Something Party had in his eyes intimidated the three of them. The barber at the third barber's station stopped outlining his client's hair and gave Party an unintimidated look, as Party came charging his way. His client knew better and got up.

Party was built like an NFL running back. He had wide shoulders, powerful arms and legs, and chiseled abs. He could do over one hundred push ups straight, before his arms would begin to tighten. He could do two hundred sit ups straight, pause, then do two hundred more, without breaking a sweat. With an uncle that was an ex-Navy Seal, Party had been groomed for volatile predicaments of all magnitudes.

The barber at the third station had been working at the barber shop, since the prior summer. He was from Southwest Philadelphia. His name was Brian, but everyone called him Briz. He was a lot taller than Party, and six years his senior. The tattoos on his face, and his thick beard gave him a tough look, but that didn't matter to Party. His uncle had taught him to only pay close attention to the eyes of a man.

As Party picked up speed, and went climbing up the barber chair at the fourth station, he saw the first glimpse of fear flash across Briz's face. Party decided to use the barber chair to even the height difference between him and the taller man. With one powerful step, he jumped from the barber chair at Briz with a flying knee. Camille and the other barbers all flinched at the cracking sound of Party's knee making contact with Briz's face. Briz melted to the floor, with Party throwing a combination of punches at him. His outliner clippers hit the base of the barber chair, and cracked into two pieces. Party stood over Briz's unconscious body with his hands still balled into fists, tempted to strangle Briz with the cord of his broken clippers.

"When he wake up, tell him he fired," Party ordered, as he approached Camille and took his guns back from her. After tucking his guns into the front pockets of his jeans, he reached into his jacket pocket and pulled out Ashley's cell phone. "That's ya cousin cell phone. We havin' a meetin' tomorrow mornin'. If you don't show up, I'll take that to mean you don't wanna work here no more. Take the rest of the day off. If any of them customers come back, before y'all leave, let them know their haircuts free for a month. It'll come outta my pockets. Now, y'all can take what I'm about to say how y'all want. If I find out one of y'all tryna line me up for my mom, I'ma kill everybody on ya father side of ya family. Dogs and everything."

Outside, Party looked up and down Marshall street, before he climbed into his truck. Camille ran out after him as he was powering his cell phone on. Party sighed and gave her a questioning stare.

"Party, can I come wit'chu?"

"What?"

"Can I come wit'chu?"

"Why?"

"So we can fuck. You got me so turned on right now."

"Seriously? You saw what I went through yesterday, right? You know what would be hilarious, though, Camille?"

"What?"

"If you was on my mom team, and this moment right here, was what got me to fall in her trap."

"Party, I don't know who that lady is. I just got this job—"

"Camille, I'ma virgin, but pussy still ain't gon' be my downfall. Not this young nigga. Not today anyway. Get them niggaz out my shop and close up."

Camille watched Party's Range Rover as it pulled out of the parking space and sped down Marshall street. No one had ever turned her down before. Men drooled over her. Upset, she ran across Marshall street and hopped into her Nissan Murano. Party wasn't going to get away from her that easy, especially now that she knew he was a virgin.

Stalker.

Chapter Seven

"Party, sometimes, the helping hand that you're looking for, is at the end of your own arm."

Party stared teary-eyed at the screen of his iPhone. The face-time moment he was sharing with his uncle wasn't providing him with the cures his heart was hoping to find. His uncle had no idea that he had been kidnapped, or that he had committed murder. It wasn't something that Party felt comfortable with discussing over the phone. Last night, he had called his sister-in-law, and she had nearly lost it. He had explained everything to her when she came to his house, and like Party had expected, his sister-in-law had instantaneously developed a newfound respect for him.

Party had always known that his sister-in-law had loved him, and had looked at him like he was her very own younger brother, but yesterday, when she had shown up at his house, he had seen just how much his life had meant to her. She continuously cried, and couldn't stop hugging him. Together, they had watched the news, and both saw the carnage left behind at the building on 8th and Dauphin that Party had escaped. The identities of the two women found dead had been withheld, until their families were notified. Party was relieved to find out that Khalid and

Murf had gotten away, but the thought of the three women also making an escape didn't sit well with him.

The possibility that the unknown women might plan another abduction had concerned Party's sister-in-law. Party, however, hoped they would. The potential threat had him excited.

The next morning, Party left his house, wearing a bulletproof vest, and carrying two guns. He arrived at his barbershop before anyone else, opened it up, anticipating danger, and looking forward to the meeting he had planned with his employees. If no one showed up, like he had explained to his sister-in-law, he was going to put up a 'Help Wanted' sign in the front window. Party was sure that Camille would be coming to work. Yesterday, after leaving the barbershop, he had spotted her following him, while he sat at a red light at the intersection of Broad and Spring Garden. Party had jumped out of his truck, and had confronted Camille, embarrassing her, and had left her there, crying, and looking stupid.

Party's older brother had no knowledge about what had happened to Party. Party's sister-in-law had called up to the prison, where he was housed, since he hadn't called at his normal afternoon, and evening times, and his counselor had informed her that the prison was on lockdown, and would be, for another day.

It was Valentine's Day, and the barbershop and hair salon was packed. Gusty winds and frigid temperatures had remained for most of the day, and had moved into the night. After the meeting with his employees, with his sister-in-law also present, Party had returned home to get some rest. A little after the sun had set, Party had awakened, showered, dressed, and returned to his barbershop. While driving, he had sent his uncle in Boston the request to facetime with him.

"How's business at your shop coming along?"

"Good. It's crowded right now. I had a meetin' with all the employees this mornin'. It went well."

"Structure is always important, Party."

"I know."

"You or Sabreena hear from your brother today?"

"Not yet. Breen called up there yesterday, since he ain't call, and they told her the jail was on lockdown."

"When he call, Party, make sure you let him know that Salvatore Masino is on his way to Philly. He'll know what to do."

"Who is he?"

"Salvatore Masino? An old friend of your father's. A solid guy."

"I never heard you say nothin' about him before."

"I had my reasons."

Party stared at his uncle's face on his iPhone for a long moment. His uncle stared back.

"Why you and Sab always keepin' stuff from me, Uncle Sko?"

"Because certain things were always better left unsaid. You was young, Party."

"Well, what about when I got older?"

Party's uncle sighed and looked away. Party checked his rearview mirror. He was parked across from the barbershop, between Camille's SUV, and a car that belonged to one of the barber's.

"The next time you and Sabreena visit your brother, ask him that same question."

"Why I gotta ask him? You can tell me right now."

"Party, Sab has always wanted to be the person who filled in all of the missing pieces for you. This was our agreement when you was brought to me. My job was to make sure what happened to your father didn't happen to–"

Party frowned and rudely ended the face-time with his uncle, then tossed his cell phone over to his passenger seat.

He glared at his cell phone, as he shifted uncomfortably to readjust the left shoulder strap of his bulletproof vest. He considered calling his uncle back and venting all of his frustrations to him, but then decided against it.

"Always treatin' me like I'ma fuckin' kid," Party thought, as he let out a long sigh of frustration, and brung his attention to the line of cars passing by. Anticipating that his uncle would call back, he angrily reached over and powered his cell phone off, then shoved it down into his pocket. "Wait 'til they find out what I did. I ain't little no more. Sab thought I ain't have it in me to kill somebody. Now, I gotta show him I can sell drugs. Daddy business is mine, just as much as it is his. Breen gon' introduce me to Salvatore Masino. Damn . . . who that?"

Party's thoughts were distracted by an attractive, young, woman, who was entering the barbershop. She was smiling and talking on her cell phone, and Party could see that all of the men in the barber shop had perked up at her presence. After zipping up his Moncler vest, Party hopped out of his Range Rover, and after a passing car went by, he speed-walked across Marshall street to his barbershop.

Inside of the barbershop, which Party quickly realized was a lot more crowded than he had initially thought, Party discreetly shot a glance to the back as the young woman was disappearing down the hallway, heading to the hair salon. Camille was watching him.

"Party, a package came for you, while you was gone."

Party gave Camille and the package on the counter an incredulous look. Interested, Party stepped around Camille and joined her behind the all-glass, reception counter, where Camille often sat, if she wasn't busy with a client, washing their hair.

"Who it come from?"

"Open it and see."

Camille followed Party's stare to the medium-sized, white box. A pink ribbon was wrapped around it, tied into a bow on top. It was sitting alone, at the far end of the reception counter, beside the mirrored wall.

"Party, Briz came by here with all these guys."

"When?"

"Right after you left this mornin'. I would've called you, but I don't have your number. Ashley said she was gon' text Breen."

"Who he talk to?"

"Well, him and Lambo never got along, so Lambo and Pooch went outside to the car they came in. I don't know what was said, but Briz didn't look happy when he pulled off."

Threats.

The barbershop was buzzing with several conversations. None of them were as loud, or seemed as humorous, as the one being held between Lambo and Pooch. The two barbers had earned Party's respect at their earlier meeting. They seemed protective of him. They both knew his older brother, which also helped with his view of their status. Lambo and Pooch's barber stations were directly beside each other, and from opening, until closing, the two barbers cut hair, and entertained. Both barbers were parolees, and had been cellmates at an upstate, Pennsylvania prison, where Party's older brother was currently being housed.

Pooch was from the Kensington section of Philadelphia, and had gone to jail for third degree murder. He was Puerto Rican, short, and he had a thin build. He had a thick, full beard, and although his face often displayed a friendly smile, his temper wasn't nothing to play with. While Camille watched, recording everything on her cell phone, Pooch had dragged Briz's unconscious body out of the barbershop by his feet yesterday.

Lambo had laughed the entire time, while packing all of Briz's barber's equipment. He had never liked Briz, and was happy to see him go. Lambo was tall, had a brown complexion, and a medium build. He wore glasses, which were usually a designer pair, and he kept his hair short and wavy, and like Pooch, he had a thick, full beard. Lambo was born and raised in North Philadelphia, and proudly represented Fairhill and Alleghany. Him and Pooch were both Muslim, and in their late twenties.

Jay was the manager of the barbershop, but he was also a barber. He was at the last station. Jay was forty-five and ran the barbershop like he was everyone's uncle, and sometimes, even their father. When he talked, everyone usually listened. The fight between Party and Briz had upset him, but Jay had known better than to get in the middle of two men fighting. At the meeting, Jay and Party had discussed the incident. Jay, like Lambo and Pooch, had clarified that Party's mother was no ally of his. Jay was from West Philadelphia, and had spent some time in prison as well. He had been caught with a gun one night, after leaving his girlfriend's house in the Logan section of Philadelphia. Jay was a few inches shy of six feet, and other than him having a big stomach, he had a muscular shape to him. Like Lambo and Pooch, Jay was also Muslim, and had a thick, full beard. He had a light complexion, and he loved to talk about anything that had to do with religion, politics, or old school Hip Hop. His topics usually started heated discussions, between barbers and customers, and anyone in earshot with an opinion.

The atmosphere in the barbershop was always unpredictable, and the conversations were never for the ears of a young child. Tonight, Party was seeing and hearing just how unpredictable the atmosphere in his barbershop actually was.

"Nigga, Briz hand wasn't better than mine. He couldn't do nothin' better than me. He can't piss straighter than me.

He don't get better bitches than me. He can't spit farther than me. Pooch, the nigga can't stand in the fuckin' shade longer than me. I'm Lamborghini!"

Shaking his head, Party looked down the length of the barber shop to the empty barber's station that Briz once occupied, as he grabbed his package from the counter. The music was loud, and everyone seemed to be enjoying themselves. Party could feel them watching him when he came from around the counter and started walking to the back. Camille's stare was obvious, but everyone else's were sneaky. What he had done to Briz was being discussed, before he had walked through the door. Passing Lambo's barber's station, Party gave Lambo a head nod, which earned him one in return.

Camille waited until Party was passing the soda machine, and almost at the hallway, leading to the bathrooms, and the hair salon, before she started to follow him. Her eyes had desire in them. She was wearing a yellow, Chanel sweater, and a tight pair of jeans. All of the men in the barbershop began watching the sway of her curvy hips as she walked; some discreetly, some openly. Camille was the reason why many of the older men came to the barbershop.

Camille tapped Party on the shoulder and giggled just as Party was about to twist the doorknob on the hair salon's door. The two of them were far enough into the hallway, to be out of sight from anyone up front in the barbershop. Party turned around and faced Camille. The smell of her perfume gave his lungs goosebumps.

"Can I have five minutes?"

"Come on, Camille," Party sighed, switching the package under his left arm over to his right. His insides skipped warm, and instantly became smoldering hot when Camille pressed her body up against his and kissed him seductively on the lips. "Five minutes for what?"

"Let me show you."

Party let Camille lead him by the hand into the employees bathroom. His erection was pressing against the fabric of his faded, Balmain jeans. The discipline to deny Camille's advances had vanished, and as the darkness of the bathroom presented itself, Party could feel his hormones doing high-fives.

Camille made sure the bathroom door was locked, before she lowered the lid on the toilet seat, and sat down. There was a hint of a smile on her face, as she finger-combed her hair and placed her Chanel sneakers on the outside of Party's Timberland boots. She was feeling giddy and anxious.

"Party, come closer. I'm not gon' bite."

Party felt butterflies scattering around in his stomach, as he was placing the package someone had sent him on the sink.

"I'm just gon' suck ya dick, okay? Party, if you like it, I'll do it everyday."

"Alright."

"I'll do it as many times as you want, Party. Come here."

Party swallowed the lump in his throat and took a nervous step forward. The butterflies in his stomach started flying up to his chest. His heart was playing tunes and skipping beats. When Camille reached for his belt, and began to unfasten it, Party thought about the two guns on his waist and grabbed her by her wrists. Before he could decide, whether he should sit the guns in the sink, or down on the floor, the unexpected and alarming sound of gunshots invaded his and Camille's secret moment. A bullet came exploding through the mirror above the sink, and exited through the upper-right corner of the bathroom door. After dropping down to a knee, Party brought his forearm up to his face. The bullet had grazed the bridge of his nose. The burning sensation was immediate, and so intense, it was causing his eyes to water. He could feel blood dripping from the graze wound, and trickling down the side of his nose.

A second bullet crashed through the mirror, and struck another hole in the bathroom door. Camille flinched and huddled closer to Party, having no idea of how dangerously close he had just come to losing his young life. The sounds of hurried footsteps, frantic yelling, and someone screaming out for help, because they had been shot, was mixing in with the unrelenting flow of gunshots. Camille started whispering a prayer. Her eyes shot a frightened glance at the bathroom door when someone tried twisting the knob to gain entry.

Pandemonium.

Eyes closed, Party continued counting the gunshots. He had reached thirty, and had settled on the gun being shot as an assault rifle. As he rose, Party wiped his forearm across his face to clean away the blood. The attempt had only smeared the blood from his nose, over to his left ear.

Camille screamed for Party to stay with her, as he unlocked the bathroom door, and went rushing out into the hallway. There were spots of blood from Party's face on the laces of one of her sneakers, and on the left sleeve of her sweater. Still afraid, and even more now, because of Party's absence, Camille moved to reach for the doorknob on the bathroom door. The moment her hand grabbed it, and she tried to pull the door closed, someone out in the hallway grabbed the outside doorknob and yanked the bathroom door in their direction. Camille released the doorknob and let out a loud scream.

Horrors.

Out in the hallway, Party ran into a stampede. Men of all ages, and sizes, were getting shoved against the walls, and those that had fallen, were down on the floor of the hallway, being trampled and stepped over. The men were fleeing from the barber shop, and heading for the safety of the hair salon. Hot bullets with no names were chasing them all. Party helped an elderly man back to his feet, and kept him by his side, as the chaotic flow of the stampede moved them both through the hair salon's open doorway.

In the hair salon, the yells and screams were gut wrenching, and just an octave beneath being hellish. Someone in the hair salon had opened the rear door, and everyone was scrambling in its direction, and piling out of it. The women in the hair salon had left behind pocketbooks, cell phones, weave tracks, and the unsightly vision of a middle-aged, Jamaican woman, who had been sitting at the first hair stylist's station. The back of her head, and pieces of her brain was splattered on the mirror behind her. The woman's eyes were open, still staring up at the TV.

The horrible image of the dead woman was etching itself into Party's memory, as he joined everyone else outside. Their were several circles of people, all of them holding panicked conversations. The rear, parking lot was dark. Again, Party used the sleeve of his shirt to wipe away the blood dripping down his face, before removing the guns from his waist and taking off in a full sprint. Someone behind him in the crowd shouted that Briz was the person out in front shooting into the barber shop. Party started running faster.

The shooting suddenly stopped, and the night became still and quiet, but only for a moment. The sound of a car fleeing the scene was heard, and then the noise of police sirens off in the distance followed.

Party caught the sight of the dark SUV, speeding down Marshall street, as he came running through the opening of a vacant lot. Without hesitation, Party rushed up the street to his Range Rover and quickly climbed inside and started it. A glance at his barber shop instantly made him sick to his stomach. The sidewalk was littered with spent shell casings, and shattered glass was all over. Inside of the barber shop, there was a teenager slumped to his side in the first barber's chair, missing the left side of his face.

Enraged, Party pulled out of the parking space, whispering tunes of murder. He stomped his foot on the gas pedal, flooring it. The needle on the dashboard of his Range Rover jerked across to the opposite side of the speedometer. In less than eight seconds, Party was down at the corner of Marshall and Popular, and was able to catch a look of the dark SUV just as it was making a left turn up at 9th and Popular.

Prey.

Beneath the Septa bridge, Briz scrambled quickly out of the passenger side of his cousin's Dodge Durango, leaving the door ajar. He ran across 9th Street like a blur. With his fast steps, Briz was removing the clip from his cousin's SKS assault rifle, and preparing to toss the murder weapon into the vacant lot's waist-high grass he was approaching. The assault rifle was empty and no longer useful. Briz ran three feet into the tall grass, then stopped and looked around quickly. He couldn't decide if he should toss the gun and clip further to the back of the vacant lot, or if where he was standing would do. His heart was beating at a pace that was feeling unhealthy to him. The ambulance and police sirens were echoing under the Septa bridge, haunting Briz's conscious with the fearful thoughts of going away to prison for the rest of his life.

Briz tossed the assault rifle to his left, then sent the clip following it. He never wanted to see the gun again. Briz removed the leather gloves from his hands like they were on fire, and dropped them at his feet, and spun around. The sight of Party running towards him with two guns aimed at his chest made his bladder weak.

Caught.

Party used the gun in his left hand to kill Briz. He put three bullets in Briz's chest, and five in his neck and face. The eight gunshots echoed beneath the Septa bridge with tremendous roars. Briz's cousin watched Party turn around and focus his attention on him with a stare that was both cold and deadly. Party ran across 9th Street to the SUV, shooting the gun in his right hand. He shot several times at the SUV's passenger side, front tire, and its back tire, then, provoked by a thrill for murder, Party dove into the SUV through the open passenger door. With no difficulty, Party started unloading both of his guns into Briz's cousin's face and head. Backing out of the SUV, he shot the dead man in his torso, until he had no more bullets in either gun.

Predator.

Unleashed.

Chapter Eight

"The woman was identified as Geraldine Sampson. As for the male teenager, his identity is still being withheld by authorities, until his family is notified. There were reports of shots fired just after five, late this after . . ."

Victoria Beauvais thumbed the mute button on her remote control to silence her TV, then she sat it beside her naked thigh. Victoria Beauvais continued staring ominously across her dark bedroom at her TV, thinking deeply about her youngest son, and the special package she had sent to his barber shop the prior afternoon. It was seconds from being 4:45 in the morning, and Victoria hadn't gotten any sleep. The violent shooting at her son's barber shop had been re-airing all night on all of the local, news stations, and the drama had her dark mind intrigued and entertained.

"Ms. Victoria, can I go home, now?"

"Not until I say you can."

"Well, can I at least answer my phone, or return some of my messages?"

"Are any of them from my son?"

"No, but–"

"Hush!"

Silence.

"When I decide to give you permission, you can do whatever your heart desires. Until then, be seen and not heard. We clear?"

"Yes."

"Good."

Control.

Victoria Beauvais let out a satisfied sigh as her Burmese python slithered over her thighs, and slowly across her flat stomach. Her clit and nipples simultaneously became sensitive from the contact of the reptile's skin against her own.

Camille was experiencing two fears; one for Party's mother, and one for the ten foot snake that was in bed with her. Camille's eyes dropped down to the screen of her cell phone. She had over fifty missed calls, and twice that amount of messages and alerts on her social media pages. A teardrop crept out of her right eye and slowly made its way down her face.

"Camille, where is the package I gave you for my son?"

"In my car."

Victoria locked eyes with Camille and gave her a long stare. The darkness of her bedroom gave her gray eyes an intimidating gleam.

"Ms. Victoria, I did what'chu told me to do. I gave it to him. He had it. I swear to God, Ms. Victoria. The shootin' messed everything up."

"I don't tolerate failure, Camille. You have one more chance to prove yourself to me. Don't fail me again."

"So, I–I can leave, now?"

"Yes . . . after you get undressed and eat my pussy."

Chapter Nine

Liberty, Storm, and Nasha, filed out of the North Philadelphia church, and down its steps in unison. All three women were visibly overcome with grief and powerful emotions. The early morning funeral was for their friend, Nadeerah.

Down on the sidewalk, Nasha slammed a fist into the hood of a parked car and began to sob uncontrollably. Liberty and Storm stood beside her, consoling her by rubbing her back.

"Liberty, I can't go to the cemetery."

Liberty and Storm looked at each other, then looked at Nasha. Nasha had been dealing with the deaths of their friends the hardest, and with each funeral, she had grown more emotionally fragile. Liberty was becoming concerned. Storm watched Liberty as she stared at the traffic flowing north and south on Broad Street, certain in her mind that Liberty was seriously considering doing something deadly to Nasha. Liberty brung her gaze back to Storm, before taking Nasha by the hand and leading her away from the church.

In.

Too.

Deep.

Raindrops started hitting the windshield of Nasha'a rented, Chevy Malibu, as she drove through the intersection of 8th and Diamond. Because Liberty had oddly chosen to sit in the backseat, Storm was absolutely sure that Liberty was about to murder their childhood friend. At 4th and Diamond, Nasha made a right turn, crying as she drove. Au 4th and Berks, Nasha pulled into an open parking space and locked eyes with Liberty in the rearview mirror.

"Liberty, when we was in the fifth grade, I had this bizarre dream about'chu. It was the night, after me and you got into that fight in Nadeerah's basement. Lib, in my dream, you killed me."

Liberty didn't blink. Her heart was crying her tears instead. Continuing to hold Nasha's stare in the rearview mirror, a sense of sadness was pulling at the fiber of her soul for the thoughts she intended on acting out. In one calm motion, Liberty pulled her gun out of her pocketbook and pointed it at the side of Storm's face. This caused Nasha's eyes to widen in shock and disbelief.

"Was Storm in it?" Liberty asked, using her thumb to cock the hammer on her 9mm Smith & Wesson. The action itself squeezed at her heart, as Storm turned to face her with tears in her eyes, and no idea what was happening, written in her facial expression. "She's the one that's going to kill you. That's the only way she'll get out of this car alive."

"Storm, no. Storm, don't listen to her."

Storm looked into Nasha's watery eyes, watching some of her tears fall, and watching Liberty raise her cell phone up to her ear with her free hand out of her peripheral vision. The barrel of the gun that Liberty had aimed at her face was only inches away. Traffic was going back and forth on Berks Street, and pass them, down 4th Street, oblivious to the tense scenario going on inside of their car. Nasha cut her eyes at Liberty when she began to talk into her cell phone. Storm slowly moved her right arm, going for the Glock 40 on her waist. All three friends had, worn 'black to their friend's funeral.

Eulogies.

"You got that text I sent. We at fourth and Berks. Me and Storm need you to come pick us up. Pedal to the metal."

"Liberty, what can I do to stop you from doin' this?"

"Nothin'. When you see Jackie, Mya, and Nadeerah, tell them I'm sorry. Hurry up, Storm."

Liberty lowered her gun from Storm's face and returned it to her pocketbook, and without looking at Nasha or Storm, she climbed out of the backseat, shut the door, and went walking in the direction of the northwest corner of 4th and Berks. Her red hair was pulled back into a neat ponytail, and the wind was causing it to dance around her dark, beautiful face. She was only standing at the corner for a few seconds, before a black, Dodge Challenger, came screeching to the curb in front of her.

The driver of the Dodge Challenger smiled at Liberty, until he noticed the tears in her eyes. As Liberty walked around the front of the Dodge Challenger, a single gunshot rang out. Storm exited the Chevy Malibu a moment later, walking with no sense of urgency in her stride.

Liberty watched Storm from the passenger seat of her friend's car closely. Storm's eyes were flowing with tears.

"Before you know it, you ain't gon' have no friends left, Liberty."

"It might be better that way," Liberty replied, opening the door for Storm, and leaning forward, so she could climb into the backseat. The moment the door was shut, her friend sped away in a hurry. "You okay, Storm?"

"Am I okay?"

"Bitch, that's what I asked, ain't it!"

"Liberty, what 'chu think?!'"

"Well, I would think you'd understand why she had to go!"

The Dodge Challenger made a hard turn down American Street, heading south. The driver kept silent, as Liberty and Storm continued to argue. He knew that being in their company was something to appreciate.

Storm placed her Glock on the backseat and started to cry, covering her face with her hands. The temptation to empty her gun into Liberty's body was present, but her ability to do it was being stopped by fear. It was an idea of inferiority that had lived in her, since her and Liberty had been little girls.

"Guilt was fuckin' with Nasha, Storm," Liberty explained, feeling no regret for insisting that Storm kill their remaining living friend. She looked through the rain-wet, windshield, as her friend drove up Girard Avenue. "Go up to Marshall Street, and a make a left. You see how she was actin' with Jackie's mom at the cemetery the other day? None of their family's know that we was there when they got killed. It has to stay that way, Storm. Nasha was gettin' weak. It's just me and you, now. The less distractions we have, the better. Our focus is that bitch, Victoria, and definitely her fuckin' son. We're movin' out to Splash's house, too. I'm pickin' up the keys from his aunt this afternoon."

"Why?"

Liberty held back her answer as her friend, Jamal, began to make a slow, left turn off of Girard Avenue, and onto Marshall Street. Storm looked out of the rear, driver's side window, and stared out at Party's hair salon. As the Dodge Challenger coasted by, Liberty, Storm, and their friend, all stayed quiet for a moment. There was still yellow police tape, on the door of the barber shop, and going across the sidewalk to a parking meter, and back across the sidewalk on its opposite side. The front windows of the barber shop was covered with huge sheets of wood. On the pavement, stuffed animals and candles had been placed in memory of the victims there. A police car was parked in front of the barber shop, occupied by a white, female officer.

"Storm, did he see you?"

"I doubt it. It was dark, and it was so many of us in the back parkin' lot. The way he came runnin' out, I thought he had got shot, too. Then, he just took off runnin'."

"Mal, make a right when we get down to Popular, and drive up to Ninth Street."

Liberty and Storm were both sharing similar thoughts as their friend followed Liberty's instructions, and made a right turn at Popular Street. Last night, like everyone else in the rear parking lot of the barber shop, Storm had also heard the gunshots coming from somewhere nearby. While the cops and detectives had all been busy responding to the aftermath of what Briz had done at the barber shop, there had also been an equally heavy police presence beneath the Septa bridge.

"We underestimated him, Storm," Liberty admitted, looking out of the Dodge Challenger's windshield, as Jamal pulled slowly up to the intersection of 9th and Popular. She looked at all of the white circles marked in the street, indicating where Party's spent shell casings had fallen. "Yeah, he a shooter. Somebody taught him the shit he know, Storm. And nobody told the cops he was there last night, huh?"

"The barbers prepped everybody, before the cops came."

"Mal, take us to my mom house."

"Alright."

"Storm, we movin' out Splash house."

"Why?"

"Rock 'n Roll Rhonda survived that situation. We both know what that mean. Storm, when they open that barber shop back up, I want you to get in there, and get that nigga under your thumb."

"Okay."

"I got an angle for y'all."

Liberty cut her eyes at her friend, Jamal, as he drove away from 9th and Popular. His eyes were flashing and dancing with mischief, as he met Liberty's stare.

"How can you help us, Mal?"

"Alright, look, that shit wit'cha cousin on y'all. I ain't gettin' in the middle of no family beef. I'm talkin' 'bout the nigga that own that barber shop."

"Okay . . . what about him?"

"His brother up Smithfield wit' my man, Reem. They on the same block. They just came off of lockdown the other day."

"And?"

"We find out who his brother celly is."

"And do what? Can you just cut to the fuckin' part, where what 'chu sayin' make sense? Damn, Mal."

"I guarantee you, his little brother be sending him pictures up there. His chick, too. Look at the envelopes."

"Their addresses?"

"Exactly."

"And how can we be sure that his celly will go through his stuff?"

"Let me handle that part. My man, Reem, a gat. His 'go' button been broke, since his mom died. The nigga got life, with nothin' to lose."

Chapter Ten

"Rhonda, how many of them pills you took this mornin'?"

"Enough to stop the pain, Zay," Rock 'n Roll Rhonda answered irritably, as she stared out of the passenger window up at the cloudy sky. She hoped her cousin wasn't about to lecture her again about her suspicions that she was slowly becoming dependent upon her pain medication. "You still ain't tell me where we goin'."

"It's a surprise."

"For me, or for them?"

"You."

"Well, if it ain't Liberty, or them two, washed up bitches, Yasmeen Bey, or Victoria, you can get off at the next exit, and turn around."

Zainab let out a sigh as she used her right hand to flip up her face veil. There was an accident up ahead on the I-95 expressway, so all of the northbound lanes were moving at a pace a lot slower than Zainab would have preferred. The traffic was stop-and-go.

Despite there being few people she now trusted, and having not the slightest idea of where her cousin was taking her, Rock 'n Roll Rhonda felt safe enough to close her eyes. The three Percocets she had taken forty-five minutes earlier were beginning to make her drowsy. The pain medication had easily been killing two birds with one stone. Her mental and emotional suffering, on most days, seemed to be competing with her physical agony. Unless her mind tormented her with a nightmare, sleep had become Rock 'n Roll Rhonda's place to escape her harsh realities.

"Zay, I'm about to stop coverin'."

"What?"

Iblees.

"Why?"

"Only for a little while," Rock 'n Roll Rhonda explained, opening her eyes to look over at her cousin. There was judgement in her cousin's eyes, and a sentiment of disappointment that she hoped her next words would cause to disappear. "Zay, once I'm fully recovered, I'm gon' be on some shit. I been thinkin' about it, since the first day I woke up in that doctor's house. I don't want my bullshit to reflect on every Muslim sister in Philly, or anywhere else, Zay. This country treat us bad enough, as it is. Shit, we already got too many odds against us, 'cause we black. With a kimar, niqab, and a overgarment, the bullseye on our backs just get fuckin' bigger, Zay."

Zainab didn't respond. Instead, she rolled her eyes at Rock 'n Roll Rhonda, and in a show of her commitment to their religion, she proudly pulled her face veil back down over her face. Her brown eyes were watery as they stared out through the windshield at the dozens of vehicles on the I-95 expressway ahead of her.

"Being in this car don't feel funny to you, Zay?"

"A little."

The 2010 Chevy Camaro belonged to the husband of their deceased cousin, Tia. The toddler asleep behind them in the car seat was his son. Splash, their deceased cousin's husband, was now their enemy, a family dynamic that at times, was still difficult to wrap their minds around.

"Rhonda, Paradise is surrounded by hardships, and the Hellfire is surrounded by–"

"Ease."

"Ma sha Allah. Right? The greater the hardship, the greater the reward. How else will Allah know who is worthy of Paradise, if He don't test us? Rhonda, don't turn to disobedience when the hardships come. You have to turn to Allah. Like, come on. Don't do this to me. Correction, don't do this to yourself."

"They gotta pay, Zay. Every last one of them."

"They will. Insha Allah, they will."

"Zay, I'm takin' a nap. Wake me up when we–"

"Rhonda, I need you to stay woke."

"For what?"

"Do I really need to answer that question? We at war."

"Who we gon' see on I-ninety-five, Zay?" Rock 'n Roll Rhonda questioned, leaning the side of her head against the passenger side window. Her eyelids had gotten too heavy to keep open, and the fight to stay awake had become futile. "Yasmeen Bey and Victoria the last people we gon' run into. Splash in jail. The cops lookin' for Liberty, for killin' Nasha. She not around. So, who I gotta stay woke for? Now, I can see, if you was worried about runnin' into my fuckin' probation officer. That bitch probably got wet when she, um, saw that viral, um, video they . . ."

Rock 'n Roll Rhonda dozed off. Zainab rolled her eyes as she looked up at the rearview mirror. Her little cousin was in his car seat, sleeping peacefully. By a show of force, she had become his guardian. She was certain that with so many unbelievable and shocking truths coming to light, her deceased cousin, Tia, would have wanted her to have her son.

"Zay?"

"Oh, now, you woke again?"

85

"If I ever go back in front of that judge, he gon' send me upstate, ain't he?"

"I thought 'chu was takin' a nap?"

"Come on, Zay. Can you just—"

"Let's cross that bridge when we get there, Insha Allah. For now, stay woke for me."

"Not that again. Zay, for who?"

"Anybody."

"So, you just want me up, starin' at random cars?" Rock 'n Roll Rhonda asked, pulling a gun from her left, jacket pocket, and then another one from her right one. With both guns in her lap, she yawned as she sat up and stared out at the traffic on the expressway. "Okay, I'm on duty, Zay. Starin' at random cars. Zay, was that—Them percs got me trippin'. Zay?!"

"What?! What's wrong?!"

"That gold BMW! Right there, Zay! Zay, that's fuckin'— Zay, that's Victoria in that BMW that just passed us! Let me out!"

Bullseye.

Almost instantly, Rock 'n Roll Rhonda introduced terror to all of the northbound lanes on the I-95 expressway, sending all of the motorists into a wave of panic. All of the vehicles that were able to move, started heading for the Cottman Avenue off-ramp.

Victoria Beauvais had abandoned her car and was running ahead of the cars for her life down the off-ramp. The very sight of her uncle's murderer had caused Rock 'n Roll Rhonda to sober up immediately. She was feeling too upset to listen to her cousin, who had wanted her to stay inside of the car. Revenge was the only emotion that Rock 'n Roll Rhonda was hoping to satisfy as she ran and climbed up on the hood of Victoria Beauvais' BMW. The rear window of the car had exploded from her first five bullets. One of the hot bullets had burned through the driver's headrest, as Victoria Beauvais was turning and pushing her door open to bail out of her car. That same bullet had burst through the windshield, and had slammed into the left, brake light, of the car Victoria Beauvais had been discreetly following.

Party and his sister-in-law were both alarmed at the sound of the gunshots, and at the noise of one hitting Party's car. They both had immediately drawn their guns. With the way that things were going in Party's life, he had quickly assumed that he was being targeted. What was more outrageous, and shocking for both Party, and his sister-in-law, was the sight of his mother running up the expressway, and down the Cottman Avenue off-ramp, dodging cars, and ducking bullets. When the Muslim woman, who was shooting at his mother ran up and climbed on the trunk of his car, and then onto his roof, Party resisted the urge to press the barrel of his gun to the roof, and start shooting through it. As the thought lingered, Party succumbed to another more inspiring impulse, and hurried out of his new Porsche Panamera, after putting it into park for his sister-in-law to take over.

Strangers, but together, Rock 'n Roll Rhonda and Party both threw bullets at Victoria. The melee became a level more intense when an off-duty cop scrambled out of his stalled pick-up truck, raising his badge and his gun. His gun was aimed at Party.

"Drop the gun!! Now!!!"

"Shit," Rock 'n Roll Rhonda cursed inwardly, quickly putting the gun in her left hand back into her jacket pocket, then using that same hand to pull down her face veil. Limping over to the guard-rail, she lowered her gun in her right hand, and watched angrily as Victoria Beauvais escaped. "You lucky bitch!!!"

"Hey?!! You, too!!! Gun down!! Hands in the–"

There were a myriad of ways that Rock 'n Roll Rhonda could have reacted when the off-duty police officer shouted his command, and aimed his gun at her. There was over sixty-five feet of expressway separating them, and hundreds of feet south of them, speeding vehicles were heading their way, totally unaware of the chaos going on.

Zainab knew her cousin extremely well. The moment she saw Rock 'n Roll Rhonda pulling down her face veil, Zainab knew then that the situation on the expressway was really about to take a tragic turn for the worse. Zainab saw all of the traffic approaching in the rearview mirror and slammed her foot on the gas pedal. Anything illegal done in the Chevy Camaro would lead back to her deceased cousin's husband. It was why she had held onto the car, and had been hiding it in a friend's garage in the first place. Racing ahead, Zainab shot a concerned look into the backseat at her little cousin, and was surprised to see that he hadn't awakened.

Rock 'n Roll Rhonda wasn't surrendering to the off-duty police officer. She took in a deep breath, and as she exhaled it, she started firing the gun in her right hand at him, while raising her left hand and flipping up her middle finger. Party took off running. His sister-in-law and Zainab were both racing their way.

Limping backwards, in the direction of the Cottman Avenue off-ramp, Rock 'n Roll Rhonda pulled her second gun from her pocket. The off-duty police officer scrambled to the other side of his pick-up truck, but continued to trade bullets with her. The bullet wound on the back of her leg had reopened, and she could feel fresh blood as it trickled down the back of her knee and over her calf. Out of her peripheral vision, she saw Party hurry into the Porsche Panamera. As it sped away, and down the Cottman Avenue off-ramp, Zainab came screeching to a stop behind her. When Zainab reached over and pushed the passenger door open for her, Rock 'n Roll Rhonda sent another hail of bullets at the off-duty police officer, before climbing in.

"Well, there goes not wanting to put a bullseye on the back of every sister in Philly!!"

"What was I supposed to do, Zay?! It was her!"

"We got Sooly in the car, Rhonda!"

Reckless.

"I forgot."

Chapter Eleven

Turbulence.

"Rhonda, this–what we dealin' with . . . it's much bigger than this personal vendetta of yours to avenge Uncle Tuna."

"Really?" Rock 'n Roll Rhonda argued, while removing her face-veil and kimar. With an irritated sigh, she pulled her overgarment up her body and up over her head, and placed it on the toilet seat with her kimar and face-veil. "Like I don't know that already. Zay, this shit about a lot of fuckin' vendettas. Mine, yours, Tia's, Kyzer's, Brittany's, Camay's, Bayyinah's. Victoria just a fuckin' bullet in a full clip for me, Zay."

"You need to worry about recuperating first. It's blood on the back–"

"I know, Zay. Why you think I asked them where the bathroom was?"

Zainab rolled her eyes at Rock 'n Roll Rhonda as she raised her ringing cell phone to her ear and accepted the call. After rolling her eyes back, Rock 'n Roll Rhonda stepped up to the vanity mirror and stared at her reflection. She smiled at the reflection of her little cousin, who was perched on Zainab's left hip. He had been watching her the entire time they had been in the bathroom. His gray eyes lit up and he smiled when he noticed that she was looking at him.

"What's my name?"

"Wock 'n Woll."

Zainab rolled her eyes at Rock 'n Roll Rhonda again and switched their little cousin to her opposite hip. She refused to call Rock 'n Roll Rhonda by her infamous nickname, and she didn't like that Rock 'n Roll Rhonda had somehow taught their little cousin to repeat it.

"Somebody wanna talk to you."

"Who?"

"The person I was takin' you to. Hurry and get yourself together. We don't know these people like that."

Rock 'n Roll Rhonda accepted her cousin's cell phone, but she didn't place it to her ear until after she was alone in the bathroom. With her free hand, she unfastened her belt, and undid her jeans, so she could inspect the gunshot wound on the back of her right thigh. The doctor in Allentown who Zainab had taken her to had advised her not to stay on her feet too much, and to get as much rest as possible. The advice had gone in one ear and out the other.

"Hello?"

"What happened to that promise you made me?"

Rock 'n Roll Rhonda frowned at her reflection in the mirror, as she held her cousin's cell phone to her ear. Slowly, she used her fingers to gradually get her jeans over her curvy hips, and down her thighs. Suddenly, she stood erect. The unfamiliar voice had taken a moment to resonate.

"Kyzer?!"

"All fuckin' day long. What the fuck is goin' on, man?"

"Wait a minute," Rock 'n Roll Rhonda winced, as she switched the cell phone to her other ear, and used her right hand to slowly reapply the adhesive tape that was keeping the gauze pad over her gunshot wound. She hissed as a layer of scab was torn from her skin with the gauze pad. "A bitch against all odds—wait. Why Zay said the person on the phone, is who she was takin' me to?"

" 'Cause, I'm home. I got out yesterday. The grand jury dropped all the charges. I'm on my way to y'all right now. Yo, you shot out."

"How? Why you say that?"

"Man, go turn on the fuckin' TV. I thought I was goofy. You burnt bacon for real."

So.

It.

Begins.

The incident on the I-95 expressway was being aired on all of the local news channels. Several police helicopters, and a news station's helicopter, were above the scene, but also showing the area of Cottman Avenue, where Rock 'n Roll Rhonda and Zainab had abandoned the Chevy Camaro. Victoria Beauvais' BMW, and the Mercedes Benz, belonging to the off-duty police officer, had been removed from the northbound lanes by tow trucks.

Rock 'n Roll Rhonda stood silently, staring from the doorway of the large, living area of the King of Prussia home, Victoria's daughter-in-law and son, had brought her and Zainab to. Luckily for her and Zainab, Victoria's daughter-in-law and son had offered them a way to escape a likely arrest. During the tense escape, Victoria's son, Party, and her daughter- in-law, had explained who they were, and Party had filled Rock 'n Roll Rhonda in on the women who had paid to have him kidnapped, and had impersonated being her. The news had caused Rock 'n Roll Rhonda and Zainab to share a knowing stare. It exposed to them how sinister their cousin, Liberty, was willing to be, in order to find Party's mother, but to also put Rock 'n Roll Rhonda's name in the crossfire.

As Rock 'n Roll Rhonda watched the 'Breaking News' with everyone else, although they were all unaware of her presence, she began to comprehend the severity of her impulsive behavior. Exactly what she had been hoping to avoid, was now staring her in the face. The off-duty police officer's description of the female shooter was vague, but damaging; a young, black, woman, wearing black, Muslim clothing. This wasn't good at all.

Party was first to notice that Rock 'n Roll Rhonda had joined them. He walked over to her with admiration and genuine concern in his eyes. If it hadn't been for her, he would have easily been arrested, or weakened to the temptation of shooting at the off-duty police officer himself.

"You okay?"

Rock 'n Roll Rhonda nodded her head as she eyed Party skeptically. He was the son of her uncle's murderer, and she was internally feeling conflicted with a few different theories of how she felt about him as a person. Her eyes went across the living room to his sister-in-law, who she immediately observed was watching her conversation with Party.

"I need two favors from you."

"Alright."

"I haven't even told you what I wanted, yet."

"It don't matter," Party clarified, holding Rock 'n Roll Rhonda's stare intently. Without her kimar, face-veil, and overgarments, she reminded him of Lauren London, and he was drawn to her for a reason he didn't quite understand. "You got me outta that situation with that cop. I owe you. So, what's the two favors?"

Zainab's cell phone started ringing in Rock 'n Roll Rhonda's pocket. Hearing her cell phone, Zainab picked up her little cousin's car seat, her pocketbook, and hoisted her little cousin up to her waist, and went heading for the front door. Their ride had arrived.

"Wock 'n Woll, we leavin'. Come on."

"Here I come," Rock 'n Roll Rhonda answered, giving her little cousin a smile as he looked over Zainab's shoulder at her. Turning back to Party, she became serious again, as she handed him her kimar, face-veil, and overgarment. "This is my first favor. Get rid of this stuff for me. You might wanna take that hoodie off, and take a hot shower. Trash the hoody with my stuff. The shower will get that gun powder residue off of you. How old are you?"

"Eighteen."

"If you wanna live to see nineteen, and stay free, leave your mom to me. Deal?"

Party took Rock 'n Roll Rhonda's things and held them under his arm. He gave her no answer.

"Do we have a deal?"

"I just thought of a better one. Deal with my mom, and I'll deal with the cousin that crossed you."

"How?"

"Don't she gotta friend named Storm?"

"Yeah. Why?"

"Before that drama kicked off at my barber shop, she came in there. She was in the hair salon."

"How you know it was her?"

"Instagram. Her page is open, so I got to see all of her pictures. Your cousin was in a lot of them, too. Since they killed they other friend, people on social media been sharin' all of these old school pictures of them. She don't know that I know it's her."

"Okay . . ."

"If what happened today don't get me caught up, and some other shit I did don't catch up to me, I'm opening my shop back up. If that bitch come through, I'll slow walk her for you."

Rock 'n Roll Rhonda smiled.

"While she think she got one up on me, I'll be rockin' her to sleep. Do we have a deal?"

"Abso-fuckin-lutely."

Chapter Twelve

A month later . . .
Rock 'n Roll Rhonda stopped and started jogging in place, as her friend, Kyzer, dropped down to the gravel path of the jogging trail to do a set of push-ups. They were about a half a mile away from Kyzer's house in Yardley, Pa., beneath the afternoon sky. Rock 'n Roll Rhonda had her hair pulled back into a neat ponytail, and was wearing a lavender, Nike sweat suit, and a pair of Nike running sneakers. A concealed Glock 40 was resting in the ankle holster down on her right leg.

Once Kyzer completed his set of fifty push-ups, he rose, and began to jog in place. On cue, Rock 'n Roll Rhonda dropped down and did twenty-five push-ups, then quickly rose back to her feet.

"Alright, you ready?"

The moment Rock 'n Roll Rhonda nodded her head, Kyzer took off running. Rock 'n Roll Rhonda shook her head and grinned as she bolted into a fast sprint. As she closed the distance between her and Kyzer, the pride she felt in her progress made her push herself harder. She had come a long way. The end of the jogging trail was just up ahead, and this time, she wanted to reach it, without being out of breath, or needing to rest her hands on her knees.

Like Kyzer had guaranteed, the afternoon jogs had been both mentally, and emotionally, therapeutic. It had also been healthy for her spirit

Rock 'n Roll Rhonda pumped her arms and legs, running as hard and as fast as she was able to. Kyzer looked over his shoulder and gave her a proud smile as they made it to the end of the jogging trail, but it was when they got there, that Kyzer watched Rock 'n Roll Rhonda closely.

"That's right, Rock 'n Roll. Head up, inhale through ya nostrils, and out 'cha mouth."

Hands on her hips, Rock' 'n Roll Rhonda inhaled through her nose and out of her mouth, as she walked in a circle around Kyzer. He was nodding his head at her with approval.

"I can't believe I did it. Damn, that felt good."

"You always had it in you."

"Yeah, right," Rock 'n Roll Rhonda exclaimed, after a heavy breath and giving Kyzer a high-five. Her mind thought about a hot shower, as they turned and began to walk back to Kyzer's car. "That first week, I ain't have nothin' in me, but complaints and excuses. Remember that night you came running to my room when I woke up screamin', 'cause I woke up with that charley horse?"

"Yo, I ain't know what the fuck was gain' on."

"Where you get that gun from so fast, is what I wanna know?"

"From under my fuckin' pillow."

Rock 'n Roll Rhonda and Kyzer shared a long laugh together, until Kyzer's cell phone started to ring in the pocket of his Under Armour sweat suit jacket. While Kyzer talked on his cell phone, Rock 'n Roll Rhonda walked beside him in silence. The longer she lived with Kyzer, the more difficult it was becoming to be in his company. She knew that he looked at her like a little sister, but he didn't know that she looked at him like the boyfriend she had always wanted, but never had. Her deceased cousin, Tia, was the only person who had known about her crush on Kyzer. She had spilled the secret to her cousin at Kyzer's sixteenth birthday party. Their families had been closely connected for as far back as Rock 'n Roll Rhonda could remember. Kyzer's deceased, sister, Camay, and her deceased cousin, Tia, had been like sisters. At Kyzer's car, Rock 'n Roll Rhonda held Kyzer's stare as he ended his phone call, and gave her a big smile. Rock 'n Roll Rhonda felt her insides melt.

"Guess who that was?"

"Who?"

"That nigga from Detroit."

"The one in the cell with Splash?"

"Yup."

"What he want?"

"He just gave me some news we can use."

"Like what?"

"Liberty and Splash engaged."

"What?!"

"That shit sound nutty, right? Her and Storm live at his house, too. That's where they hidin' out at."

"Oh, really?"

"Guess what else, though?"

"What?"

Kyzer pulled open the driver's side door to his black, Cadillac ATS, and ducked inside. Anxious to hear more, Rock 'n Roll Rhonda snatched the passenger's side door open and hurriedly ducked inside too. She looked at Kyzer with growing anticipation.

"Kyzer, what else?"

"I think we should go out to that house and holla at them nut ass bitches. Tonight."

"I couldn't agree more."

Family.

Feud.

8:14 p.m.

The sun had set, and Rock 'n Roll Rhonda's temper had risen. Her mood for murder was encompassing all of her thoughts. At times, random teardrops had escaped her brown eyes, as reflection on her life had swung her emotions and dark thinking to areas of her past that no one knew still bothered her. Rock 'n Roll Rhonda had never stopped mourning her parents. As an only child, she had been the only witness to all of the domestic violence that went on in her house. Her father had been a traveling con artist, and had been well aware that Rock 'n Roll Rhonda's mother dated successful drug dealers, only to deliver their secrets to her brothers, who would later rob them. Rock 'n Roll Rhonda's father had been a jealous man, and at times, his insecurities would cause big disputes.

It was a phone call on the Thanksgiving of 2002, that had disturbed their peaceful dinner. As her mother giggled, while talking on her cell phone, Rock 'n Roll Rhonda's father's eyes had become evil. Her parents had argued and fought for hours. The gunshot had awakened Rock 'n Roll Rhonda from her sleep. She had discovered the lifeless bodies of her parents in their bedroom.

Rock 'n Roll Rhonda let out a sigh and blinked away the horrible images of her dead parents, and saw Kyzer standing there in the doorway of his guest bedroom she had made her new safe haven. Being alone in Kyzer's house with him for an entire month had helped her to understand so much more about his personality. Still, like her, he had his days and moments when he spent most of his time inside of his master bedroom, and was less talkative.

"Did Zay text you the passcodes to they alarm system, yet?"

"Yeah," Rock 'n Roll Rhonda replied, as she rose from the bed and zipped up her black, Givenchy jacket. She took her black gloves from the bed, stuck one in each jacket pocket, then headed for the bedroom doorway. "Our problem is, Zay not sure if Liberty changed it once she got there. If you ask me, that can leave us on the outside of that big ass house, lookin' like fools."

"Well, it's only one fuckin' way to find out."

"And you know, since that situation with Zay and that Haitian nigga, and what he did to Brittany, if just one of them rich, white people see us creepin' around that—"

"This me and you, right?"

Rock 'n Roll Rhonda stopped in front of Kyzer out in the hallway and gave him a nod, as she looked up into his serious eyes. He had on a black scully, hiding his long braids, and pulled down close to his eyebrows. All of his clothes were black, and his Dior Homme sneakers were dark blue. She wondered what type of gun he was carrying for their trip.

"If we on anybody top, only Allah can save them. Alone, we deadly. Tonight, we about to find out how diabolical we can get as a team."

"Kyzer, this bitch gotta pay."

"Alright, let's get to it, then. Make this bitch cry, before she die."

"Fuck her tears. I wanna bury that dumb, red-headed bitch alive."

"Sounds like a plan to me."

Rock 'n Roll Rhonda and Kyzer were quiet the entire drive out to Chestnut Hill. Rock 'n Roll Rhonda had spent the time thinking, as she stared out of the passenger window. She once cut her eyes at Kyzer, wondering if visiting her deceased cousin's house would bother him in any way, since his girlfriend had been violently killed at the house a few months ago, before he had been arrested.

Once they arrived, Kyzer circled the upscale community twice, before finding a safe place to park. The dark sky made their silent approach to the lawn of the mini-mansion an easy one.

Rock 'n Roll Rhonda and Kyzer dropped down to the grass, and they both began to bear-crawl across the lawn. It took them less than a minute to reach the front of the giant house, and with alert eyes, and some slightly accelerated breathing, they quickly sat between two manicured bushes that were beneath a window.

"While we in there, I got somebody to help with diggin' that bitch grave."

"Who?"

"I'll introduce y'all when that time come. So, how the fuck that alarm system work again?"

"By voice, or handprint," Rock 'n Roll Rhonda explained, leaning forward to look over at the front door of the mini-mansion. Her anxiety went up a few levels, as she rose from sitting to a squatting position. "I was here when it got switched. Tia and Splash got it, after Tia's brother, Angelo, and they cousin, Mikey, got by the old one. This one more high-tech. The front door can open two ways. If you in the system, you can either put your palm on that clear screen thing, and the door will unlock for you, or, just say the password into that little speaker."

"What Zay said the passcode to get in was?"

"Snookums."

Rock 'n Roll Rhonda smirked when Kyzer gave her a weird look at hearing the passcode.

"Snookums, though? What the fuck is that?"

"That was Tia's dog."

"It's a dog in there?"

"It died a month after Tia did."

"Damn."

"Okay, so, here's our problem. Every window in the house, and the doors, have these metal curtains that can come down, if the house get put on lockdown-mode, Kyzer."

"Yeah?"

Rock 'n Roll Rhonda nodded her head, as Kyzer slowly turned to stare back at the window they were squatting beneath. He brung his eyes back to hers, seemingly uninterested with the threat of possibly being imprisoned inside of the big house, once they were inside.

"Alright, so, what we gon' keep sittin' out here like some fuckin' lawn furniture, or we in there?"

"Follow me," Rock 'n Roll Rhonda ordered, as she stood and led the way up to the mini-mansion's front door. She bit on her lower lip as she pulled open the screen door, grabbed the front door's knob, and leaned her face extremely close to the small speaker beside the doorbell. "Snookums."

Rock 'n Roll Rhonda held her breath after she spoke, and to her astonishment, and Kyzer's, who was standing closely behind her, the doorknob slackened in Rock 'n Roll Rhonda's right hand, and she was able to push the front door open. Rock 'n Roll Rhonda and Kyzer pulled out their guns, before they took another step.

Adaptations.

Liberty sat up in bed and looked around. Her eyes did a full circle, going from the open doorway of the master bedroom, to the master bathroom's closed door, over to the massive, walk-in closet, over all three bedroom windows, and back to the master bedroom's open doorway. Liberty wasn't sure what had awakened her. With a sigh, Liberty grabbed her cell phone and called her friend, Storm.

"I'll be there in about an hour."

"Where you at?"

"Onyx."

"With who?"

"Who you think? He never been to a strip club before."

"He tell you where he live, yet?"

"I'm hopin' I'll find out tonight. What's wrong? I thought 'chu was tired and had a headache?"

Liberty could barely hear Storm's voice over the loud music in the background. An odd noise from somewhere in the house made her give the open doorway of the master bedroom a curious look. The lights were out, and the only light in the bedroom was the glow of her cell phone. Sensing that something was wrong, Liberty ended her call with Storm, and quickly sent her a text message, letting her know that she thought that someone else was in the house with her. Liberty swung her legs out of bed, grabbed her gun from the nightstand, and went to investigate. Her cell phone made a pinging sound, notifying her that Storm had responded to her text message as she moved through the darkness out of the bedroom.

Rock 'n Roll Rhonda and Kyzer had split up. Rock 'n Roll Rhonda knew the house like the back of her hand. It had been passed down to her cousin, Tia, from her aunt, Quintessa. The circumstances that Liberty were there under made Rock 'n Roll Rhonda's blood boil. Her cousin's betrayal had no boundaries for the living, or the dead. Rock 'n Roll Rhonda got to the top of the spiral staircase, and turned right, aiming her Glock in the direction of the master bedroom.

Down the opposite end of the hallway, Liberty was staring down at Kyzer through the plexiglass floor of the office. Her eyes followed Kyzer as he moved stealthily through the home theater, and towards the doorway that led to the kitchen. Liberty wanted to meet the intruder and kill him, but with her mind only on him, she nearly screamed out in shock when she ran head-on into another intruder out in the hallway.

Liberty was no match for Rock 'n Roll Rhonda, and because she had dropped her gun when they had collided, she quickly made a feeble attempt to surrender by throwing her hands up in the air. It wasn't until she realized that the intruder was actually her cousin, that she dove to the floor after her gun.

"Yeah, it's me, bitch!" Rock 'n Roll Rhonda shouted, sweeping Liberty's gun behind her with one of her feet. With that same foot, she kicked Liberty in the face, and with a soaring rage that was engulfing all of her senses, she started pistol-whipping her cousin with her gun. "Don't ball up, bitch! !Fight me! Fight me back! !Fight me back!! You . . . disgraceful . . . bitch! !All I did for you?!!"

Rock 'n Roll Rhonda's yelling was echoing around the entire mini-mansion. Kyzer followed her voice, aiming his gun with two hands at the darkness ahead of him. He came walking from the opposite end of the long hallway.

"Yo, she out! Rock 'n Roll, she out!! Look . . . yo, she not even fightin' you back no more!"

Rock 'n Roll Rhonda ignored Kyzer and continued to pistol-whip her cousin viciously. She was straddled on Liberty's stomach. She had a handful of her red hair, and was using her other hand to deliver punishing blows with the handle of her Glock. When Rock 'n Roll Rhonda felt her right arm getting tired, she switched the gun to her left hand and started beating Liberty's face some more.

Kyzer pulled out his cell phone and tapped the screen several times, sending a text message. Out of caution, he took a peek into the office. His eyes were immediately drawn to the plexiglass floor. When Rock 'n Roll Rhonda stood, breathing heavily, he met her stare with raised eyebrows.

"Gimme a zip-tie."

Kyzer handed Rock 'n Roll Rhonda a zip-tie from his back pocket. As Rock 'n Roll Rhonda secured Liberty's hands behind her back, Kyzer walked over to Liberty's gun and picked it up. Before putting it on his waist, he looked at it and checked the clip.

"You checked that room down there already?"

"Yeah," Rock 'n Roll Rhonda assured, looking at the blood that was on the backs of her gloves and on the sleeves of her jacket. She took in another deep breath to calm her breathing, as she rested her eyes on her cousin's motionless body. "I caught her comin' outta the office. For her to have that gun, she must've heard one of us. Unless, she was in the office when we first came in, and she saw you goin' through the home theater. Watch her for me, while I go find her phone."

"My man 'n 'em on they way, so they can do that diggin' for you."

"Where should we take her?"

"The fuckin' backyard cool wit' me. Leave her as a gift for Splash."

Minutes later, Rock 'n Roll Rhonda and Kyzer were both staring at the screen of Liberty's cell phone, going through her pictures, and her text messages. They were waiting for Liberty's friend, Storm, to respond to a text message Rock 'n Roll Rhonda had sent her. Eight minutes earlier, Storm had sent a text message, asking Liberty was everything okay. Seeing the text message that Liberty had sent Storm, notifying her that she suspected that someone was there at the house, Rock 'n Roll Rhonda wanted to keep Liberty's friend at ease.

Kyzer turned and faced the wall in the long hallway that had been made into a 20 foot wide, fish tank. It was impossible to ignore. There were so many beautiful, and colorful, freshwater fish. The interior light of the aquarium was providing a pinkish-glow, reflecting from the pink gravel at the bottom of the fish tank.

"Kyzer, look."

Rock 'n Roll Rhonda held up Liberty's cell phone for Kyzer to see the screen. Liberty's friend had sent her a new picture. In the picture, Party was getting a lap dance from two strippers at the same time. Party was raining money over their heads, and smiling from ear to ear.

"If only she knew."

"After tonight, she'll be the last one left," Rock 'n Roll Rhonda acknowledged, pocketing her cousin's cell phone. When Liberty's body showed a subtle movement down at the other end of the hallway, she pulled her gun from her waist and took quick steps in her direction, angry, and poisoned with hatred. "Wake up, bitch. So, you been up in here, tryin' to be Tia, huh?!You and Splash don't get enough, do y'all? Do y'all, bitch?!"

Liberty groaned in pain, and blinked open the only eye of hers that could. She tried swallowing, and instantly began to choke when two of her broken teeth scraped at the back of her throat.

"They here, Rock 'n Roll."

Liberty turned her face in the direction of the voice. Her left eye was swollen, but not fully closed like her right eye. She felt a tremble in her chest when she recognized the face of the male intruder.

"Hey, Lib. It sucks to be you right now, don't it?"

"Kyzer, tell them to get started," Rock 'n Roll Rhonda instructed, as she watched Liberty stare at Kyzer. She knew her cousin was processing things, and as she did, it was providing her with a gratifying rush. "It's double-doors down in the kitchen that let out to the yard. Can you go open them for me?"

"Alright, but let me help you carry her down the steps first."

"This bitch ain't gettin' no preferential treatment. I'm gon' make sure this ginger-bitch head hit every fuckin' spiral step goin' down. You can do me a favor, though."

"What?"

"Use another zip-tie for her ankles."

"Got 'chu."

Once Rock 'n Roll Rhonda was left alone with Liberty, she glared down at her for a long moment. Memories of their childhood came and went, as Liberty's sobbing echoed up and down the dark hallway.

Liberty started to sob harder when Rock 'n Roll Rhonda grabbed her by both ankles, and started to drag her. The carpet beneath her was burning the skin on her back and shoulders, but this pain was on a level far lower than the mental and emotional agony she was dealing with, in knowing that her final moments alive were growing shorter with each step that her cousin took.

"I'm sorry!! Rhonda, I'm sorry!!!"

Liberty's apologies only made Rock 'n Roll Rhonda angrier. At the end of the hallway, Rock 'n Roll Rhonda unloosened her grip around Liberty's ankles, and hooked her fingers around the zip-tie that had Liberty's ankles bound together. Just as she took a step backward, and placed her left foot on the top spiral step, Liberty yelled out a word in Spanish that took Rock 'n Roll Rhonda by surprise, and caused her to stop. There was suddenly a soft humming noise that seemed to be growing with momentum all around the house. Once Rock 'n Roll Rhonda realized what was going on, it was too late.

Simultaneously, two-inch sheets of metal came down and protectively sealed every window and door on the first level of the mini-mansion. A second later, the same happened with all of the windows on the second level of the giant house.

"Let me live, and I'll let 'chu out."

Rock 'n Roll Rhonda looked down at Liberty speechless, as she released the zip-tie, and let Liberty's feet fall down to the floor.

"You and Zay know the passcode that don't matter. Splash gave me the one that do."

Chapter Thirteen

Lockdown.
12:19 a.m.
Chestnut Hill, Pa.

"Keep diggin'," Rock 'n Roll Rhonda ordered, before switching her cell phone to her opposite ear. She kept her voice low, as she paced down at the other end of the hallway, looking over her shoulder at her cousin."Kyzer, this bitch goin' in that fuckin' grave. Tonight. They almost done?"

"Pretty much. Somethin' told me to keep my ass in there wit'chu."

A sinister thought came to Rock 'n Roll Rhonda's mind as she stared down the hallway at her cousin. She cursed at herself silently, because the idea hadn't come to her thoughts a lot sooner. In a hurry, she pulled out her cousin's cell phone, and began going through her contacts.

"Kyzer?"

"Talk to me."

"Get that grave ready. I'll be out there in fifteen minutes."

"We'll be done in ten."

Once Rock 'n Roll Rhonda found the contact in Liberty's cell phone that she was looking for, she called the contact. On the first attempt, she was sent to voice mail.

On the second attempt, her call was answered on the third ring.

"Yo, Lib?"

"Try again."

Silence.

Rock 'n Roll Rhonda activated the speaker on Liberty's cell phone as she walked down the hallway to her. At a light switch, she paused and flipped it up.

"Splash, you sunk to an all-time low," Rock 'n Roll Rhonda spoke, as she squatted next to her cousin and back-handed her with the handle of her gun. She glared at her cousin with contempt." How many of my cousins you tryna fuck, Splash? Recognize the voice, yet? You do."

Silence.

"Tia would be so disappointed in you," Rock 'n Roll Rhonda continued, as she pushed the nozzle of her gun into Liberty's left eye socket. When she tried to move her face away, she tapped the barrel of her gun roughly on her forehead. "So, I'm in this fabulous house that my aunt built. The one my cousin opened up to you. The one you decided to let my other cousin come play house in. Splash, the best cousin you had from my family dead. Liberty could never walk in Tia's shoes. Not in five lifetimes."

"Bitch, I don't give a fuck about none of y'all."

"Clearly. I know that. You been showed Zay that. Do Liberty know that, though? I know what 'chu do care about, though."

"Tia dead. She all I ever fuckin' cared about. And my son."

"Well, Sooly can't be used against you. He's my cousin."

"Exactly. So, it ain't nobody you can use against me. Fuck all of y'all."

"You hear that, Lib?" Rock 'n Roll Rhonda smiled, happy that her cousin was overhearing these selfish words from a man she had betrayed their family for. Her smile went away when her cousin let out a whimper. "You wasn't nothin' to him, but a fuckin' pawn. He used ya dumb ass! He can't protect you, if he wanted to! Where he at, Lib?! This Tia house! She never needed him! Aunt Tessa made sure Tia was set for life! She had it all, before his stupid ass even came into her life!"

"And I added to what she already had, bitch! Rock 'n Roll, my story ain't over! Y'all keep thinkin' that!"

Mr. Gunplay.

"How would you feel, if you came home, and your dad's truck wasn't in the garage?"

Silence.

"Tia told me all about the special connection you have with that truck, Splash."

"Don't touch that truck, Rock 'n Roll. I swear to fuckin'–"

"Splash, she–I got her locked inside the house," Liberty whimpered, unwilling to accept that she meant nothing to Splash, and wanting him to know that the two of them still had the upper hand. Her face and head was battered and bruised, and each time she opened her mouth to speak, the right side of her face exploded with shocking pain. "I–I said the lockdown-word, Splash. She can't go nowhere. Um, Splash, Kyzer here with her. They tryna take me somewhere."

Rock 'n Roll Rhonda picked up Liberty's cell phone, and took it off the speaker. Placing it to her ear, she didn't speak, until she was further down the hallway, away from Liberty.

"Tell me the passcode, and I'll leave your father's truck alone."

"Or, I can hang up, and make some calls."

"To who?"

"Rock 'n Roll, this me. I'm locked up, not washed up. I can have that house surrounded wit' killers, before you can spell Barack Obama name."

"Pussy, B-A-R-A-C-K . . . O-B-A-M-A. Where they at?"

Silence.

"The passcode, Splash?"

Silence.

"Splash, the fuckin' passcode? Don't make me go down to that fuckin' garage with some lighter fluid."

"It's grandmother, in Spanish."

"I don't know how to say that shit. I'm gon' put'chu on speaker. You say it for me."

Rock 'n Roll Rhonda activated the speaker accessory on Liberty's cell phone once more, and she held the cell phone up in the air.

"Awwaleeta."

Liberty's entire body tensed at hearing Splash say the passcode. Her sobbing started again, and so did the light humming sound that the house had made, moments before the alarm system had sent the house into lockdown-mode.

Rock 'n Roll Rhonda walked down the hallway to Liberty with a dangerous look in her eyes. She had Liberty's cell phone in her right hand, and her gun in her left. Her approach made Liberty sob harder.

"Here's your last chance to say some last words to your fiancé, Splash."

"Fuck her, and fuck you. And tell Kyzer I fucked his sister."

"No, you didn't."

"I did. Her pussy was good, too. And Tia knew. Make sure you tell Kyzer that."

Those secrets from Splash kept echoing in Rock 'n Roll Rhonda's mind as she grabbed Liberty by the ankles and began to drag her down the spiral steps. The moment the metal sheets rose back up into the recesses above the windows and doors on the first level of the mini-mansion, Kyzer didn't waste a minute reentering the house. He stood waiting down at the bottom of the spiral stairs, until Rock 'n Roll Rhonda reached him.

"Come on, so we can get this shit over with."

"Get one of those dish rags for me from the sink. This bitch might try to scream outside."

Kyzer walked over and grabbed a dish rag from the sink, and knelt beside Liberty's motionless body and stuffed the rag into her mouth. She didn't put up a struggle. She had been knocked unconscious by one of the spiral steps.

Out in the backyard, Kyzer introduced Rock 'n Roll Rhonda to his friends, Tauheed, and Ern. Both young men were from South Philly, and had a serious attitude about them that Rock 'n Roll Rhonda quickly appreciated, as they helped her roll her cousin's body down into the shallow grave. Liberty's body landed awkwardly on her left shoulder, and the lower half of her body slowly began to settle with it.

"She just moved."

"Good," Rock 'n Roll Rhonda commented, taking the shovel from Tauheed, and walking over to the small mountain of dirt, beside the grave. She stabbed at the dirt with the shovel, gathered enough on it, turned and tossed the dirt down onto Liberty's moving body. "I want that bitch to die slow."

Kyzer had Liberty's cell phone, and was kneeling down at the foot of the grave, recording Liberty as she looked up at them. She flinched and fought with the zip-ties every time the dirt from the shovels landed on her. Rock 'n Roll Rhonda was deliberately tossing dirt at her face, while Tauheed and Ern focused on filling the space around the rest of her body. Before giving Kyzer the cell phone, Rock 'n Roll Rhonda had logged on to Liberty's Instagram account. Instantly, people were viewing the shocking burial, and posting comments.

The.

Living.

Dead.

Chapter Fourteen

Victoria crossed her left leg over her right, then lifted her expensive pocketbook from the hardwood floor and placed it on her lap. There was a look of conceit in her gray eyes as she watched Zainab come through the front door of her grandmother's West Philadelphia home. Victoria was sitting at the piano. Zainab's eyes went across the living room to Victoria, then came back to the two, tall men, who had been standing on both sides of her grandmother's front door when she entered. Their guns were aimed at her face. Zainab placed a protective hand over the back of her little cousin's curly head, and held his face against her shoulder.

"Dimitri, bring me the baby, while your brother checks her."

"Victoria, my cousin is stayin' right here with—"

"He can get shot," Victoria threatened, uncrossing her legs, and sitting her pocketbook on the piano bench, before standing. She gave the Russian brothers a nod, as she returned her attention to Zainab. "Do you want that? Him and I will sit here, while you and I talk. Or, every fuckin' bullet in Dimitri's gun can burn in that precious little body of his. You decide."

"Where's my gran'mother?"

"Where's Rock 'n Roll Rhonda? Today, we'll be tradin' a life for a life."

Chapter Fifteen

Party's house was in the Art Museum section of Philadelphia, on 30th and Popular. It had been the first piece of real estate that Party's father had ever purchased. Party's father had spared no expenses, and had invested two hundred and eighty-two thousand dollars into having the three-story property transformed into a drop-dead, palatial structure.

"Party, who designed this house?"

"Some lady my dad knew."

Storm opened her mouth to ask Party another question, as him and Camay continued with their private conversation up ahead of her. She took another tentative step, then became paralyzed, as she stared fearfully down at Party's kitchen, beneath her feet. The entire hallway on Party's second floor was a glass bridge, providing a vertiginous path above his kitchen. The walls of the hallway had been painted teal green, and in various places, there were vintage, oil paintings, and some family photos. Still walking timidly, Storm paused and stared at a framed photograph on the wall. It was an old picture of Party being held by his father, as Party's older brother stood smiling beside them. Storm was amazed at how closely Party resembled his father.

Storm's full name was Stormy Williams. Her mother had given birth to her on the floor of a bathroom in a dirty North Philadelphia bar. Her mother was a black woman addicted to crack, and her father was from the Dominican Republic, and a man who spent most of his time at the neighborhood bars, than he did at home.

Storm knew what it meant to struggle. Growing up, she had experienced several nights, where the only food she had to eat was sunflower seeds. Other than Liberty, her ex-boyfriend had been the only person she had ever truly felt loved by. Her ex-boyfriend was currently at an upstate prison, because he had beaten Storm with a lawn chair in front of Liberty's house, causing her to miscarry their unborn daughter. Liberty's mother had testified against him at his jury trial. With Liberty too now gone from her life, Storm was feeling lost. She was also fearing that she was next on Rock 'n Roll Rhonda's list. For now, she was just grateful to be alive, and relieved that Party had no idea about her original motives when they had first began to talk at his barber shop weeks earlier.

Tonight, Party had unexpectedly invited her and Camille back to his house. In the past week, the three of them had gone to several strip clubs. Storm was beginning to think that Party may have reached his sexual breaking point for a combination of reasons. As Storm slowly stepped over to look at another picture on the wall, she thought about the hot look in Party's eyes when he had watched her and Camille tongue kiss in the backseat of his Range Rover, where they had also performed oral sex on each other as he drove to the take-out restaurant in West Philadelphia. Then, there was the molly she had slipped into their bottle of champagne at the strip club, that had gone unnoticed.

"Party, why this room don't have anything in it?"

Up ahead, Party stopped and turned around. Camille followed him back to where Storm was standing. If everything went the way it seemed to be going, according to Victoria Beauvais, Party would soon be under Camille's spell, and Camille was excited. She was wearing the special lipstick that Victoria Beauvais had given her, as well as some of her perfume.

Unholy.

Alliances.

"I ain't figure out what I wanna do with it, yet," Party explained, as he stepped beside Storm and looked into his empty bedroom. His body was hot, he was intoxicated, and as he licked his lips, he smiled at Storm when she grabbed his hand and held it between both of hers." It's the only room in the house that my dad didn't fix up. I'ma leave it like it is."

"Let me see."

Party and Storm stepped aside, giving Camille space to get a good look into the empty bedroom that the two of them were talking about.

"And what's in that room at the other end of the hallway?"

"A bathroom."

"Alright, I'm outta questions. I was just stallin', 'cause this floor is really fuckin' with me right now."

"You scared of heights?"

"Camille, mind your business. Can you carry me across on your back, Party?"

Amused, Party looked from Camille, to Storm, then he followed Storm's gaze down to his hallway's glass floor. He knew exactly what Storm was feeling. It had taken him days to get comfortable with walking across the glass bridge. After first removing the two guns from his waist, and handing them over to Camille, Party squatted down in front of Storm, so she could climb onto his back. Camille gave them both a roll of her eyes, and started walking ahead of them, pointing Party's guns at fake targets.

A little while later . . .

One dick.

Two mouths.

"Party, feed it to me. I want all of it in my mouth."

Party swallowed the lump in his throat, as he fisted his hard dick with his right hand and slowly guided the head of his dick into Camille's open mouth. He instantly felt tingling sensations come to life in his balls, the backs of his thighs, his calves, and even his ankles. He let out a sigh that joined Camille's moaning, and together, their sounds made a song. Storm was kneeling beside Camille, impressed by how much of Party's dick she was able to fit into her mouth. As she continued to pleasure herself by rubbing slow circles on, and around her clit, she tilted her head and started to greedily lick and suck on Party's balls. Party bit his bottom lip and tilted his head back in total satisfaction.

The oral extravaganza was unfolding in the center of Party's bedroom. The bedroom was spectacular, and took up the entire third floor. The rear wall was a floor-to-ceiling pane of glass. Facing it, the Art Museum, and some parts of the Parkway could be seen. Party favored this part of his house more than anywhere else. It was here, where Party often stood by himself on sleepless nights, and thought about his father, his mother, and the way his own life was beginning to get the best of him.

A few feet away from where Party, Storm, and Camille, were pursuing pleasure, stood Party's gigantic, walk-in closet. It was an all glass enclosure that rose up to the ceiling on all of its three sides. Its back wall was one huge mirror. The glass closet looked like it had been air-lifted out of the men's section of a department store. It was so huge, it divided Party's master bedroom into two halves. There were four aisles in the walk-in closet, and this was the only area of the bedroom that had spotlights in the ceiling. This was also the only section of Party's master bedroom that had Pergo flooring. There was black carpet everywhere else.

Party's bed was a stainless-steel, king-sized frame, that suspended from the ceiling by four steel cables. The mattress was stuffed with Alaskan geese feathers, and the six pillows on the bed had the same type of filling.

Three feet from the head of Party's bed, there was a Jacuzzi, a walk-in shower, and a toilet, all walled in by glass. The see-through bathroom gave Party's master bedroom an alluring touch.

"Party, I wanna watch you fuck Camille."

Pussy.

"Real slow."

Pussy.

"Ain't that how you like it, Camille?"

Camille nodded her head at Storm's question, as she continued to lick and suck Party's hard dick. She grabbed his dick, lifted it, ran her tongue along the length of the bottom, paused to lick and suck on both of his balls, then offered it to Storm when she was done. Party's dick was glistening with her saliva.

"Let's get back on the bed, y'all."

Storm let Party and Camille walk ahead of her. As Party and Camille climbed onto Party's bed, Storm knelt down beside Camille's discarded clothes and grabbed one of Party's guns. Without one moment of hesitation, she took another step and fired three shots into the back of Party's head, and when Camille let out a shriek and turned to face her, Storm shot Camille once in the forehead, and twice in the neck.

Chapter Sixteen

The very second the woman pulled the driver's side door closed on the Volvo SUV, Rock 'n Roll Rhonda sat up in the backseat and pressed the barrel of her gun against the back of the woman's head. The woman's body went rigid. Rock 'n Roll Rhonda used her thumb to pull the hammer back on the Kimber 45 Kyzer had given her.

"Hand me your pocketbook. Do it slow."

The woman's eyes were fearful as she looked up at her rearview mirror, and slowly removed her pocketbook from her lap, and handed it to the stranger behind her.

"Now, pull off," Rock 'n Roll Rhonda ordered, as she sat the woman's pocketbook beside her, while meeting her eyes in the rearview mirror. The woman worked for Yasmeen Bey, and for that reason, had become an enemy by default. "And you better fuckin' drive like you got some sense. Do anything stupid, and all that make-up, and them fuckin' fake eyelashes, gon' be stuck to that dashboard with your brains. I wanna know where Yasmeen Bey at."

"She, um, I think Lydia might know. I just started workin' at that daycare center last month."

"Two days in a row, I watched you open and close that daycare center."

"That's because I live in the neighborhood."

At the intersection of 7th and Tasker, Rock 'n Roll Rhonda stole a glance out of the rear window of the Volvo to make sure that Kyzer was following them. In that split-second, the woman took her foot off the brake pedal and bailed out of her car, screaming at the top of her lungs for help, as she ran west up Tasker Street. Rock 'n Roll Rhonda cursed when the SUV began to roll across the intersection. In a hurry, she quickly climbed up to the driver's seat, stopped the SUV, put it in reverse, than jerked the steering wheel left, after putting it back in drive, and went after the fleeing woman.

It was just beginning to get dark outside, and the mostly-Italian area in South Philadelphia was empty. The woman's frantic screams was causing some neighbors to come to their doors.

Rock 'n Roll Rhonda drove the woman's SUV up onto the pavement after passing the woman, and the woman cut back out to the street, between two parked cars. An elderly man came out of his house with his cell phone to his ear, reporting to a police dispatcher what he was witnessing. Rock 'n Roll Rhonda put the Volvo in reverse, backed off the pavement, and watched as the woman climbed into Kyzer's car, believing he was a good samaritan.

The tires on Kyzer's Cadillac ATS squealed as he drove in reverse back to the intersection of 7th and Tasker. There, the black car made a sudden stop, then disappeared up 7th Street out of sight.

Rock 'n Roll Rhonda knew that if she wanted to stay a free woman, she had to think fast, and move fast. The elderly man was out in the middle of Tasker Street, watching her as he talked into his cell phone. Rock 'n Roll Rhonda kept her eyes on him in the rearview mirror as she raced the Volvo SUV up Tasker Street. At 8th Street, she made a hard right turn, and pulled wildly into an open parking space. Her heart was slamming against her chest.

Rushing, she snatched the woman's pocketbook from the backseat, stuffed all of the paperwork from the glove compartment in it, and hurried out of the SUV like the seat was on fire. Calmly, she crossed 8th Street, and pulled out her cell phone when she got to the sidewalk, and started walking south.

At Morris Street, Rock 'n Roll Rhonda turned left, still pretending to be having a serious conversation on her cell phone. A police car appeared up at the intersection of 9th and Morris, and Rock 'n Roll Rhonda felt her heart rate speed up. Rock 'n Roll Rhonda thought about several things in the moment that the police car was turning, and coming her direction. She hoped that Kyzer had gotten away safely as she slowly began to pull his gun from her waist, while staring at the approaching police car. Her eyes flared when the police car accelerated and raced by her down Morris Street, and her cell phone began to ring in her hand at the same time.

Rock 'n Roll Rhonda let out a sigh of relief, as she switched the woman's pocketbook to her other shoulder. Walking faster, she gave the unknown number on her cell phone a strange look, before she finally decided to accept the call.

"Hello?"

"Rock 'n Roll Rhonda, we need to talk. Can you not do, or say anything to anybody, until then?"

"Who this?"

"Um, your cousin, Zainab . . ."

Rock 'n Roll Rhonda stopped walking, even as the sounds of police sirens pierced the late afternoon air all around her. She hadn't heard from her cousin in two days, which was odd, but in being caught up in her own agendas of revenge, she hadn't taken a moment to see how she was doing, or if she was okay or not. Something in the young woman's voice was suddenly giving Rock 'n Roll Rhonda a bad vibe.

"She gave me your phone number. She ain't want me to call nobody else, but 'chu."

"Where she at?"

"Her gran'mother house. Can you hurry up?"

"Who this?"

"Tasha. My aunt live next door. Zainab gave me my shahadah last week. Somebody hurt Zainab real bad. We found her out in the backyard. She made us promise not to call the cops."

"I'm on my way."

There were tears in Rock 'n Roll Rhonda's eyes as she walked down the concrete steps of the Septa subway station at Broad and Morris. A southbound subway had departed moments earlier, and a small crowd of people were rushing up the steps past her. Rock 'n Roll Rhonda regarded none of them, and never lifted her watery eyes, until she stopped in front of a token machine. She inserted a five dollar bill she had fished out of the woman's pocketbook, and when the bronze tokens from the machine fell down into the small dish, she only removed one, and left the rest.

On the subway, Rock 'n Roll Rhonda sent a text-message to Kyzer. She told him about the call she had received about her cousin, and asked him to meet her at Broad and Lehigh. When the subway made its stop at the City Hall station, Rock 'n Roll Rhonda started going through the pocketbook that belonged to Yasmeen Bey's employee. She folded the woman's car registration, and her insurance paperwork, and stuck them in her pocket. Next, she went through the woman's cell phone. She searched the contact list, until she found two names she was looking for.

At the Lehigh station, Rock 'n Roll Rhonda exited the subway not knowing how she was going to hold her composure, once she got to her cousin, Zainab. With a shaky breath, she took the concrete steps in twos, and immediately began to look for Kyzer's car, once she was above ground on the Broad Street sidewalk. The sky had darkened, and it had gotten breezy. Doing a full circle, Rock 'n Roll Rhonda felt more anguish as she began to think that Kyzer might have possibly been arrested down South Philadelphia with Yasmeen Bey's employee in his car.

"It's really just me now," Rock 'n Roll Rhonda thought, as she let out a sigh and jogged across Broad street. At the other sidewalk, she walked a few feet, then tossed the pocketbook over to the wall of a building, and never looked back. "This–"

Kyzer's Cadillac ATS pulled up slowly to the curb and stopped. Rock 'n Roll Rhonda looked back at Broad Street, and back to the car as she approached the passenger door with a sad smile on her face. Her eyes went straight to the backseat when she climbed into Kyzer's car.

"Where she go?"

"My trunk. You still got some questions for her, right?"

"Yeah, but–Alright, go to third and, um, and, um, York."

Kyzer pulled his car away from the curb, leaning his left shoulder against his driver's side door. Whenever a red light stopped him on Lehigh Avenue, he gave Rock 'n Roll Rhonda a thoughtful look. He kept doing this, until she pointed it out.

"I wouldn't be doin' all this for a lot of people, Rock 'n Roll."

"Well, since you puttin' that out there, why are you?"

"Our history. Your heart. Mine."

Rock 'n Roll Rhonda stared into Kyzer's eyes when he looked at her, before making a right turn down American Street. He was so many men in one. She had killed his best friend. She had once been affiliated with a man Kyzer despised, and wanted to kill, and yet, he had found a way to overlook those grave mistakes.

"When I came home from that juvenile joint, I started spendin' more time down South Philly. I was meetin' all these other cousins I never knew. Then, one summer, I started goin' back up North real heavy. Plus, my excuse to my mom, was that I wanted to spend time with Drees, and my aunt."

"I wasn't in Philly back then."

"I know."

"Kyzer, I never would've done that to Hasaan, if I had've known he was so close to you. Wallahi, Kyzer. Your name was never comin' up. It was just his."

Kyzer let out a sigh as he flipped his turning signal, and made a right turn onto York Street. He wouldn't look at Rock 'n Roll Rhonda, so she turned in his passenger seat to face him as he obeyed a stop sign at the 3rd and York intersection.

"Do you believe me, Kyzer?"

Kyzer let out another sigh, as he pulled over and parked on the opposite side of 3rd Street, behind a parked, Ford Explorer. There was a couple hugging, as they leaned against the SUV's passenger door. The couple was a young, Puerto Rican woman, and a young, black guy, who seemed interested in who was inside of Kyzer's car.

"Look, I cracked that bitch in the head with my ratchet to knock her out. I'ma turn my music on a little, so if she wake up and start actin' goofy, people like these newsy mu'fuckers right here won't hear her. If it get too outta hand, I'ma bend the block."

"Can we finish our conversation later?"

"Sure. If you need me to come in, text me. I can get somebody to come and get the bitch in the trunk, and hold her, until you ready to deal with her."

"Alright."

123

As Rock 'n Roll Rhonda walked across 3rd Street, she could feel her heart twisting in her chest. She saw someone pull a curtain aside at one of the first-floor windows of Zainab's grandmother's house as she walked up the sidewalk. Zainab's grandmother was a sweet woman, who had always been judgmental of her. She was the mother of Zainab's father, and had been involved in Zainab's upbringing. The grandmother that Zainab and Rock 'n Roll Rhonda had shared, was no longer alive. At their grandmother's funeral, Ms. Thelma, Zainab's paternal grandmother, had tearfully vowed that her front door would always be open for Zainab's uncles, aunts, and cousins.

Rock 'n Roll Rhonda thought of that vow as she twisted the doorknob and walked into Zainab's grandmother's house. Inside, she lost her breath, as she looked around.

"They upstairs."

Rock 'n Roll Rhonda acknowledged the teenage girl, who was standing at a window closest to the front door. There was a gun in her hand. Tears suddenly flowing, Rock 'n Roll Rhonda pulled her own from her waist as she ran for the stairs. Fearing what she might see, she cried harder as she took the steps in twos and threes. On the second floor, she ran down the hallway and into the bedroom, where she saw Zainab's grandmother standing over a bed. Rock 'n Roll Rhonda dropped to her knees and started sobbing when she saw what had been done to her cousin.

"Rhonda, she got Sooly. It was Victoria. Uncle Tuna brung her here before."

"Why she take Sooly, Zay?"

"She wanted you. They tried to make me call you, so I could set 'chu up to come here. They had my gran'mom downstairs in a closet tied up, and wanted me to trade her life for yours."

Zainab's grandmother sat down on the bed, and gently pulled Zainab's hands into hers. While she had been bound and gagged in her downstairs closet, she had tearfully listened to the entire ordeal.

"She was by herself?"

"She had these two big Russian guys with her. They twins."

Rock 'n Roll Rhonda rose to her feet and looked down at her cousin's face. She was unrecognizable. Zainab's eyes were both swollen shut, and her right cheek bone was swollen and bruised also. There was a nasty gash running over her left eyebrow, and down across the bridge of her broken nose. Teardrops were blinding Rock 'n Roll Rhonda's eyes as Zainab reached out for her hand.

"Rhonda, you gotta get Sooly back."

"I am."

"She left a cell phone for you. It's downstairs on the kitchen table. She want 'chu to call her."

Rock 'n Roll Rhonda scrambled over to the door, then rushed back over to Zainab. Her tears fell on Zainab's face as she leaned over and placed a tender kiss on her swollen, right cheek.

"Rhonda?"

"Huh?"

"May Allah azza wa jal–"

A sob interrupted what Zainab had attempted to say. Her grandmother looked away, but quickly brung her eyes back to Zainab's face. Rock 'n Roll Rhonda stood there, gun in hand, waiting for Zainab to finish her invocation.

"May Allah azza wa jal, Ash-Shadeed . . . punish her swiftly by your hands. Ameen."

"Ameen," Rock 'n Roll Rhonda repeated, crying as she walked out of the bedroom. At the doorway, she stopped and turned. "I'ma make sure you get Sooly back, Zay. I won't come back, until then. Any enemy we ever had, I'm gettin' them outta here. Won't nobody be left. I promise."

Chapter Seventeen

"Why I'm down here?"

"You'll know in a minute. Want a cigarette?"

"I don't smoke."

"Coffee?"

"I want my lawyer," Splash requested, staring angrily at the young, white detective, as he removed the handcuffs from his wrists. The smell of coffee and cigarettes was biting at his nostrils as he gave the small interrogation room a once-over. "Give that message to whoever got me down here."

"Will do."

Splash gave the detective a contemptuous stare as he left the interrogation room, and closed the door behind him. He had no idea why he had been brought down to police headquarters from the county jail. He hadn't been a free man, or touched the streets of Philadelphia in almost four years. So much in his life had changed in that amount of time; none of it for the better.

After a half an hour of being alone, the interrogation door was pushed open, and in walked the very man who was responsible for Splash being charged for murder. Both of Splash's hands became fists. The reaction made Detective Konn smile.

"Ya nut ass got me down here?"

"I do. Off the record."

Splash frowned and turned to look up at the small camera up on the wall, pointed at where he was seated at the table.

"It's off."

"All y'all mu'fuckers corrupt. At City Hall, in here, at CJC, and the fuckin' D.A. buildin'."

Detective Konn's face became serious, as he took a seat on the opposite side of the table from Splash. He was meticulous as he made a show of separating a stack of folders he had with him. Splash watched as Detective Konn unstacked each folder and placed them side by side, until they went from one end of his side of the table, to the other. There were six folders in total.

"Rasool, the information in these folders are worth tickets to Heaven. Know why?"

"I don't care."

"You'll change your mind. Maybe, not this second, but I'm certain you will. When you're in the backseat, and those detectives are driving you back up to State Road. It could happen, while you're locked in that cell, and you can't get to sleep, no matter how hard you fuckin' try. Whenever it happens, all of this, what's right here in front of you, Rasool, will have a profound fuckin' impact upon your way of thinkin'. That, I am fuckin' sure of."

Splash had an unconvinced expression on his face, while holding Detective Konn's stare across the table. He hated the Detective with every fiber of his soul. Still, in hindsight, Splash wished he had've taken the corrupt detective's threats a lot more seriously, and simply had just paid him the bribery money he had initially been asking for.

"Take this folder, for example. Who's that with your father?"

Splash gave the top photograph a skeptical gaze as Detective Konn opened the folder wider, and turned it so that the folder was facing him. Powerful emotions began to set fires inside of his chest. He suddenly felt confused about his past, as his eyes stayed fixed on the picture of his father, who was sitting in the passenger seat of a black, Mercedes-Benz, with Trixie Masino. The two of them were kissing. Splash couldn't look away.

"There's more."

"I don't need to see more."

"This next picture will make you change your mind, Rasool."

Splash let out a sigh and looked up at the ceiling of the interrogation room, as Detective Konn shuffled the picture of his father and Trixie Masino to the bottom, and replaced it with another one.

"Have a look."

"No."

"Rasool, let me explain a few things to you. Maybe, we got off on the wrong foot. Maybe, before giving you that ultimatum at your club that afternoon, I should have simply let you in on just how powerful I am. Perhaps, then, your decision about paying me the amount of money that I asked for would have been less problematic for you."

"You bragged about killin' my fuckin' dad."

"Yeah, and you know what? Maybe, I should've kept that information to myself. It would have been a lot wiser to introduce myself with these."

Splash followed Detective Konn's left hand across the layout of folders, and stopped, when his eyes came upon the photograph that Detective Konn wanted him to see. The images in the photograph only made him more confused than he already was. He dragged his eyes off of the old photograph and looked up into Detective Konn's ugly face. The detective appeared to be pleased at his obvious discomfort.

"Who took them pictures?"

"Me, of course. I believe, when you and I first met, I told you how closely I had been following your father's career as a hitman. During his era, Philadelphia had a pretty interesting cast of characters, running its underworld. People were putting hits on people ninety going north, Rasool. Trixie Masino and your father made a lot of money together. She got the jobs, and he executed the orders."

Splash thought about each and everyone that had ever told him old stories about his father. He then replayed every conversation him and his father had held. Trixie Masino's name had never come up once, except for the time he had gotten enough courage to tell his father that he himself too had become a hitman, and that his employer was his wife's aunt, Trixie Masino. As he sat there in silence, Splash tried hard to focus his mind on that vintage conversation with his father, and if there had been a reaction from his father that he had simply ignored. Splash could remember none.

"When Victoria Beauvais showed up in Philly, the dynamics in a lot of relationships changed. Hers with her husband's. Your father's and Trixie's. Sufyan Bey's with Salvatore Masino. All hell broke loose, Rasool. There were crosses, double-crosses, and triple-crosses. You see that picture of your father with Victoria Beauvais?"

Splash glanced down at the photograph of his father with Victoria Beauvais. The two of them were sitting at a table in a restaurant, and appeared to be conspiring together. They both were wearing serious facial expressions.

"I tailed them to that restaurant one afternoon. Guess who else was there?"

Detective Konn didn't wait for an answer. He did another shuffle of the pile of photographs, and now on the top was a photograph of Trixie Masino, wearing sunglasses, and watching Splash's father, and Victoria Beauvais, from a table on the other side of the crowded restaurant.

"See, Victoria Beauvais hired your father to take out Salvatore Masino and his little brother, Carmen. She wanted her husband taken care of last. Trixie thought they were doing the hanky-panky. Now, let me tell you this, the voodoo stories you heard about her . . ."

Detective Konn used his index finger to tap the image of Victoria Beauvais' face on the photograph, as he looked intently into Splash's eyes.

". . . all true, Rasool. That pretty bitch had everybody spooked."

"Why you got me down here, showin' me all this shit?" Splash questioned, leaning back in his chair. He was certainly intrigued, but his reason for being there, and what everything Detective Konn was telling him had to do with him, was now his primary concern. "I already know my dad was in the mix. Trixie used to fuck wit' my dad and never told me. So? Victoria Beauvais was fuckin' wit' my wife uncle, and most likely knew I was my dad son. So? None of that shit concern me. Man, get them to take me back. Got me down here, lookin' at some old ass fuckin' pictures."

"There's a deal on this table for you, Rasool."

"What? A deal? Man, take me back. I ain't no fuckin' rat."

Mr. Gunplay.

Detective Konn gave Splash a pitied look as he shook his head. He moved to gather all of the folders together, but a sudden thought stopped him. He met Splash's angry stare with one of his own.

"Usually, I play with my cards close to my chest, Rasool. I have to. I mean, look at me. I'm short and ugly. Becoming a cop was the only way I could stop people from bullying me. I had that plan, since I was ten. Be a fuckin' cop. Gain power over people. I had no chance in the streets. People with my setbacks are forced to become opportunists, Rasool. It's how we survive in this world. We don't wait for opportunity to knock. We open the door and invite it in, the moment we see an opportunity on our sidewalk. I thrive off it, Rasool. Now, a few weeks ago, a car registered in your name was used by some Muslim woman, who ran into Victoria Beauvais on the expressway. Just the other night, Victoria Beauvais' youngest son, and a young female were both found dead at his house. Ironically, one of the cops from that district arrived on the scene, and he recognized Victoria Beauvais' son as being the guy who had joined in with the Muslim woman, who jumped out of your car, and had been shooting at Victoria Beauvais. Clearly, you had no way of driving your car, Rasool. I put the kibosh on them dragging you down here sooner. My power benefits me in the judicial system in ways you could only imagine."

"Well, make it work to get me the fuck out, without me rattin' on nobody."

"Will you help me find Honey?"

"Honey?"

"The stripper from your club. The one who helped that Haitian guy kidnap your wife's assistant."

Splash gave Detective Konn a strange look, as the possibility of freedom began to bombard his mind with a wide range of thoughts. Getting his son back was his first hope.

"Rasool, I'm desperate to find her."

"Why?"

"She was pregnant with my son. If you want this murder charge to go away, I'll see to it that Angelo forgets everything. For that to happen, my original price that we discussed for me to ignore your lifestyle has to be doubled. That, and I want you to stop this war between Rock 'n Roll Rhonda, and Victoria Beauvais."

"How the fuck I'm supposed to cease that?"

"Figure out a way, Rasool."

"Man, I ain't got shit to do with them."

"I've gotten involved in a lot of cases that your name was tied to, Rasool. All for this moment. The last time I heard from Honey, she told me about this plot your wife had to kill me at your club last Halloween. She's scared to come back. She was there when that Haitian guy killed your wife's assistant out in front of your house. She told me you wanted that done, Rasool. She told me how your wife's cousins are keeping your son from you. It's almost nothing I don't know. Victoria Beauvais is trying to locate a house her husband owns, because there's a lot of money hidden there. I need her to find it, Rasool. Once she does, I can make an appearance. Rock 'n Roll Rhonda is distracting her from that aim. By the way, they buried your wife's cousin in your backyard. And another thing, Victoria Beauvais' oldest son, might be your brother. Trixie Masino's hunch was spot-on. Him and Victoria Beauvais were fucking."

City.

Of.

Secrets.

Chapter Eighteen

Gray skies were covering the afternoon skies of Philadelphia as Rock 'n Roll Rhonda steered the dark colored, Acura SUV, into the entrance of the parking garage. The sidewalks and streets were still wet from a passing shower. Rock 'n Roll Rhonda was on her way to her storage unit that no one knew about.

Rock 'n Roll Rhonda was a young woman who believed in herself. She had confidence in her capabilities to do anything she put her mind to. As she parked, climbed out of the SUV, and answered her cell phone, while walking down the long aisle to her storage unit, she was kindling the rage that was growing in the pit of her stomach. She was determined to make an example out of Victoria Beauvais, once and for all.

"Kyzer?"

"Yo, look, I know we talked about it already, but before you do anything, come see me. Alright?"

Rock 'n Roll Rhonda sighed, after stopping in front of her storage unit. As she considered Kyzer's request, she tapped her storage unit key against her hip. She was ready to make the call to Victoria Beauvais, but before she did, she wanted to be properly equipped to go to war. She had made a list of people she wanted to kill. Kyzer had been right there beside her as she was writing down their names.

"You still home?"

"Naw, I been left. I'm at the Chrome Depot."

"When I'm close, I'll call you."

"Alright."

"Okay," Rock 'n Roll Rhonda replied, returning her cell phone back to her pocketbook, after ending the phone call. Stepping up to the lock on her storage unit, she unlocked it, then knelt to lift up the metal shutter. "They about to find out, who's not to be fucked with. Nobody on that list gettin' pity from me."

Rock 'n Roll Rhonda walked into her dark storage unit and pulled the metal shutter down behind her for privacy. She placed her pocketbook on the top of a waist-high safe as she walked around it. Her mind was a storm of so many violent ideas and angry thoughts. For light, she went back and dug her cell phone out of her pocketbook and aimed its light at a tall safe, standing in the far-left corner of her storage unit. Using her free hand, she punched in the passcode on the safe's keypad. A second later, she twisted the safe's brass handle and pulled open the door.

There were ten Kevlar dresses hanging inside of the safe. Rock 'n Roll Rhonda reached inside and only removed one. She walked over and laid the bulletproof dress on the safe, beside her pocketbook, then she went over to the other side of the storage unit to a pile of duffel bags, and unzipped the camouflage one sitting on top. Rock 'n Roll Rhonda's eyes danced dangerously as she slowly pulled out her hand-grenade belt. Thoughts of her deceased cousin, Tia, were adding to the deadly confidence she was feeling. Most of the arsenal in her storage unit was once hers. At another safe, Rock 'n Roll Rhonda removed fifteen Glocks, an AR-15 assault rifle, and over a dozen extra clips.

Rock 'n Roll Rhonda stood abruptly when the cell phone Victoria Beauvais left behind for her began to ring. She answered it, before it could complete its first ring.

"Hello?"

"You had specific instructions to call me. Learn to follow orders."

Tears of rage flooded Rock 'n Roll Rhonda's eyes at the sound of Victoria Beauvais' voice. Her hand that was holding onto the cell phone against her ear began to shake involuntarily.

"Where my little cousin?"

"Who killed my son?"

"I don't know. Victoria, where the fuck is my little cousin?!"

"In one of my animal cages."

Rock 'n Roll Rhonda dropped down to her knees, and covered her mouth with her hand to smother a sob.

"Answer that fuckin' phone when it ring tomorrow morning. Your little cousin's life depends on it."

"Bitch, I'm gon'—"

Victoria Beauvais ended the phone call, and Rock 'n Roll Rhonda sat there in the darkness of her storage unit, crying on the floor. Images of her little cousin being caged like an animal, all alone, confused, and frightened, was tormenting to her angry heart. It took Rock 'n Roll Rhonda almost eight minutes to regain her composure. She packed everything she came for in two duffel bags, and left her storage unit with a look in her brown eyes that held no compassion for her enemies.

Violence.

Rock 'n Roll Rhonda sent a text-message to Kyzer, once she was in North Philadelphia. As she drove east on Cecil B. Moore Avenue, she checked social media to see what was being talked about. Two nights earlier, she had created a fake Instagram account, and a Facebook account. She was currently following several people she had intentions on killing on Instagram. She was studying their habits, and paying attention to all of the places, where they would take their pictures. Ignorantly, many of them hadn't removed the GPS locator from their cell phones.

At Tenth and Cecil B. Moore, Rock 'n Roll Rhonda brought the Acura SUV to a slow stop and gave the small group of young women on rollerblades an odd look. Each woman was carrying a backpack. They too were traveling east on Cecil B. Moore Avenue, but what Rock 'n Roll Rhonda found most strange about the group of seven young women, was their facial expressions. They all seemed serious, and had concentrated looks. Rock 'n Roll Rhonda eased her foot off of the brake pedal, and purposely drove slower, so that she could watch the young women as they coasted ahead on their roller blades.

Until she reached the intersection of Eighth and Cecil B. Moore, and witnessed the young women, removing Halloween masks from their backpacks, Rock 'n Roll Rhonda simply found it odd that some young females in North Philadelphia would find enjoyment in being on roller blades on a beautiful, March afternoon. It quickly became obvious to Rock 'n Roll Rhonda that the women on roller blades were up to something malicious.

Behind her tinted windows, Rock 'n Roll Rhonda snapped a quick picture of the group of women, then sent it to Kyzer's cell phone. With the picture of the women, Rock 'n Roll Rhonda explained in a short text-message that the women had split up, with some going east on Cecil B. Moore Avenue, and three of them going south down 8th Street. When Kyzer didn't respond, Rock 'n Roll Rhonda sped up and passed the women. At the intersection of 8th and Oxford, stark realization quickly set in as Rock 'n Roll Rhonda looked up at her rearview mirror and saw the three women on roller blades pulling their Halloween masks over their heads.

Rock 'n Roll Rhonda raced the Acura SUV across the intersection and down 8th Street, while twisting and reaching into one of the duffel bags on the backseat. Kyzer and some of his friends came running down the steps of a house as she raced by. They all had guns in their hands. At Jefferson Street, Rock 'n Roll Rhonda made a sharp left, and parked in the first available parking space she saw. Her heart was beating hard and fast as she scrambled out of the SUV with her AR-15 cradled in her hands, and rushed around 8th Street.

The young women on roller blades were indeed teenagers, but they weren't inexperienced when it came to shooting guns. This wouldn't be their first time launching an attack on Kyzer. At the sight of Kyzer, the three young women pulled out their guns from their backpacks, and separated. The trio started firing their guns with a quickness that was automatic and practiced. The young woman wearing the Nicki Minaj mask continued to roller blade down the middle of 8th Street, while her two friends veered away from her to the sidewalks. They all seemed unafraid of the bullets coming their way.

Rock 'n Roll Rhonda dropped to a knee and started firing her assault rifle up the street at the young woman, who was wearing the Hillary Clinton mask. Her first spray of bullets missed, and peppered the windshield of the parked car behind her. Her next barrage of bullets hit their mark. Rock 'n Roll Rhonda watched as the young woman's left leg gave out and her body went buckling down to the pavement. After falling, she shot back down the street at Rock 'n Roll Rhonda, then began to crawl frantically for safety behind a parked mini-van. Rock 'n Roll Rhonda was forced to duck, as the driver's side mirror on a car beside her shattered into the air. The sounds of another shootout blocks away was also echoing in the late afternoon air.

The young woman wearing the Nicki Minaj mask made a sudden stop, and veered left between the parked cars, where her friend Rock 'n Roll Rhonda had shot had retreated to. From that position, she rose and ducked, trading gunshots with Kyzer and his friends. Her friend on the opposite sidewalk, had also made a sudden stop, and was using a parked mini-van as a shield. She was wearing a Marilyn Monroe mask, and shooting a handgun that had an extended clip longer than her arm.

Suddenly, two, Nissan Titan pickup trucks came fishtailing to screeching stops at both ends of Eighth Street. The one at Oxford Street came peeling down Eighth Street in reverse, and after it was halfway down the block, two men, wearing ski masks popped up from the flat-bed, and began firing assault rifles at Kyzer and his friends. The pick-up truck down at Jefferson street stayed facing forward. Its driver and Rock 'n Roll Rhonda shared a momentary stare, before he stuck his arm out of the window and started trading gunfire with her.

Police sirens could be heard in the distance, as the exchange of bullets stayed rapid and intense. Rock 'n Roll Rhonda advanced to the pickup truck that her old mentor was in, aiming her assault rifle at his windshield, hoping her bullets would find homes in his face.

Up the street, the three young women on roller blades were crawling, and shooting over their shoulders. The one that Rock 'n Roll Rhonda had shot was bleeding the entire way. Her older brother was one of the men in the back of the pickup truck, shooting an assault rifle. When he saw her, he immediately stopped firing his weapon and climbed out of the flat-bed to help her. Kyzer ran out into the middle of the street and fired his gun at the brother and sister. Their necks jerked back violently when hot bullets slammed into both of their faces. A piercing scream came from behind the mask of the young woman, wearing the

Nicki Minaj mask, as she watched the siblings fall to the ground.

Rock 'n Roll Rhonda ducked as she moved left, moving quickly away from her old mentor's line of fire. The windshield on his pickup truck was riddled with bullets. Rock 'n Roll Rhonda let the empty clip from her AR-15 fall to the ground, and immediately replaced it with another one. As Maniac, a man she once respected and looked up to, began to pull away in his pickup truck, Rock 'n Roll Rhonda struggled with the impulse to chase after him, while understanding that in a short matter of seconds, the scene was going to be flooded with police.

Hours later, Rock 'n Roll Rhonda and Kyzer were sitting on the floor in Kyzer's foyer, sharing a large pizza, and listening to music, as they talked about Victoria Beauvais' phone call that Rock 'n Roll Rhonda was to be expecting the next morning. Rock 'n Roll Rhonda had her legs crossed at the ankles, with her AR-15 beside her to her left, and her half-eaten slice of pizza on a paper plate, resting on her lap. Kyzer had his back against the same wall, but on the other side of his full-body of vintage armor, is where he sat. His face was inches away from the shiny axe that his 6'4" suit of armor was holding in its left hand.

Like Rock 'n Roll Rhonda, Kyzer's eyes were randomly shooting glances down his foyer to his front door. If anyone came through that front door, cops included, him and Rock 'n Roll Rhonda were going to shower them with enough bullets to wet their souls. Kyzer was sitting Indian-style, with the opened box of pizza closest to him, wearing a shoulder holster that held two Smith & Wesson 45s. Because the first level of his mini-mansion was a construction of glass walls, with one sweeping glance, him and Rock 'n Roll Rhonda could view his open kitchen, dining area, living room, without any visual interruptions.

Rock 'n Roll Rhonda had become comfortable staying at Kyzer's house. An hour earlier, he had stood in the doorway of his guest bedroom, seemingly sad, while watching her pack her belongings.

"Kyzer, who on my list you think I'll have the most problems with?"

"Whichever ones you underestimate. Look, you can't think that you gon' sweep through that list, wit'out no headaches. In war, you just gotta treat enemies as such. When my aunt and Drees other wife came here, makin' all them threats, it was my fault I ain't take them seriously. Yo, that shit cost me."

"Because you lost Brittany?"

Rock 'n Roll Rhonda leaned forward and looked over at Kyzer when he ignored her question. He was chewing his pizza, and staring off into space.

"Naw, I was home for that. I keep forgettin' you was locked up. When that shit happened to Brit, I was still up at that masjid in the Northeast. I'm talkin' 'bout the way I left my team. In three months, a lot of shit fell apart. Even before the cops ran in here, though, I was losin' it. I really was sick, after I found out Brittany was pregnant. In here with the lights off all day, depressed, cryin', ignorin' everybody phone calls. On some bullshit."

Rock 'n Roll Rhonda and Kyzer stopped talking for a long moment. Kyzer's digital jukebox began playing some R&B songs from the 2000s.

"Let it play, Kyzer," Rock 'n Roll Rhonda pleaded when Kyzer rose to stop the song from playing. He paused and gave her an annoyed look, as she rose to her feet too, while lip syncing the love song by Avant and Keke Wyatt. "If I never see you again, I won't be mad at allll . . . Kyzer, let's take a picture. For a memory."

At the end of Kyzer's foyer, where it opened into his kitchen, there was a photo booth, that stood beside his digital jukebox. Rock 'n Roll Rhonda grabbed Kyzer by the hand, leading him over to it, as he finished off the slice of pizza from the pizza box.

"How the fuck both of us gon' fit in there?"

"I can sit on your lap. Go 'head."

Rock 'n Roll Rhonda smirked when Kyzer's eyebrows raised at her suggestion of sitting on his lap inside the small photo booth. He was clearly uncomfortable, but with the uncertainty of what might come next in her life, over the days ahead, she wasn't about to miss the opportunity of fulfilling one of her childhood dreams.

All.

I.

Desire.

Inside the photo booth, Rock 'n Roll Rhonda and Kyzer made random facial expressions, as the photo bulb flashed. In some pictures they smiled, and in two, they both made silly faces. The moment was innocent, and definitely seemed to be, until Rock 'n Roll Rhonda grabbed Kyzer's smiling face with both hands, and kissed him gently on the lips. She felt his body tense, then gradually relax. The arm that he had around her waist pulled her closer to him, and as his eyes held her gaze, he opened his mouth and began to kiss her back.

"You sure you okay with this kind of memory?"

Rock 'n Roll Rhonda nodded as Kyzer pulled back and looked deeply into her eyes. Her lust for him was empowering every hormone in her body. Again, she initiated another kiss. This time, their kiss was a lot more sensual. Internally, she was feeling an emotional relief, because Kyzer's body language was revealing that he clearly was physically attracted to her. The notion that he wanted her equally as much had her smiling as the two of them kissed.

"What? Why you smilin'?"

"You," Rock 'n Roll Rhonda blushed, climbing off of Kyzer's lap, and stepping out of the photo booth. She sighed when she felt some wetness from her pussy, trickling down the back of her thigh. "Boy, you just don't know. Get up and follow me. This my show tonight."

Chapter Nineteen

Romance.
By.
Chance.

"Alright, this ya show. Where this goin' down at?"

"The living room," Rock 'n Roll Rhonda instructed, after reaching down and grabbing her assault rifle by its handle. With her free hand, she began to unbutton her shirt, as she walked behind Kyzer into his living room. "This been a fantasy of mine for a long time, Kyzer."

"You bullshittin'."

"My pussy gon' tell you the truth. Take off everything, except for your shoulder holster."

"What?"

"Keep your shoulder holster on. Everything else comes off. The first one naked decides our first position."

Sexual.

Revolutions.

"Well, since this memory all about 'chu, I'm gon' undress real slow."

Rock 'n Roll Rhonda smiled as Kyzer slowly pulled his hoody over his head, and dropped it to the floor. His eyes were glued to her every move, as she tossed her shirt aside, and began to unhook her bra. She held Kyzer's stare. Their eyes were doing a mating dance.

Lustful.

Conquests.

Under the amazingly high ceiling of Kyzer's living room, there was a 30 by 30 foot, white, mink rug, spread out over the center of the bamboo floors. On top of the white, animal fur, there was a white, leather sofa, a matching ottoman, and two, sycamore armchairs, all facing a gigantic movie screen. The temperature in the living room was comfortably cool from the central air, and with the lights on, Rock 'n Roll Rhonda and Kyzer were in clear view of each other's nakedness.

Rock 'n Roll Rhonda was comfortable in her own skin, and confident in how she physically looked. Her waist was small, her breasts were full and perky, and her thighs, hips, and ass, were toned, and shapely. She had soft, brown skin, and the only scar she had, was an inch and a half long scar over her left ribcage, where a bullet had grazed her three years earlier. The scar was a shade lighter than her complexion. Rock 'n Roll Rhonda was a beautiful, but dangerous woman. None of her boyfriends had ever been able to control her. The father of her infant daughter had tried unsuccessfully to rid her of her wild streak, and had even proposed to her. Sadly, the unfortunate and accidental death of their daughter, had also been the death of their relationship.

With her pussy wet, and her eyes enjoying the sight of Kyzer's naked body, Rock 'n Roll Rhonda grabbed Kyzer by the hand and led him to his couch. There, she let Kyzer take a seat first, before straddling him and intertwining her fingers behind his neck. The feeling of Kyzer's dick growing harder, longer, and thicker, as he wrapped his arms around her waist, while he began to lick slow circles around her left nipple, nearly made a scream of excitement escape her lungs. When he kissed her neck, and behind her ear next, she sighed and reached down between them to grab his dick, and put it at the opening of her pussy.

It started as a slow introduction, with Rock 'n Roll Rhonda using Kyzer's shoulders to balance herself, as she lowered herself on Kyzer's dick. The penetration felt like a hot knife slicing through butter. Rock 'n Roll Rhonda's year and a half long streak of being celibate was now officially over. As her and Kyzer were kissing like lovers, his hands were palming her ass cheeks, helping to guide her as she rose, and lowered herself on his dick. Again, and again, and again, she bounced, and gyrated her hips, letting out satisfied sighs when Kyzer interrupted their steamy kisses to suck on her titties. Her first orgasm came fast and sudden, like a thief in the night, taking a minute's worth of oxygen out of her lungs.

On unsteady legs, Rock 'n Roll Rhonda pulled Kyzer down to his mink rug. On all fours, and arching her back, she looked over her shoulder as he stroked her pussy with an attitude. He looked so sexy to her, as he held onto her hips. He had his long, curly hair, in two Indian braids. His handsome face was serious as he seemed to be putting all of his concentration into his every push and pull. Rock 'n Roll Rhonda was privately appreciating Kyzer's focus. A low moan was humming in her chest as another orgasm began to build in her core. Ready for its sensation, Rock 'n Roll Rhonda buried her face in the mink rug, arched her back some more, and the thrill she was feeling when the head of Kyzer's dick began pounding into the back of her pussy made her scream as her second orgasm tore beautiful rainbows through her vibrating body.

Rock 'n Roll Rhonda and Kyzer had sex in every position, in almost every area of his big house. Before leaving Kyzer's living room, Rock 'n Roll Rhonda had rode him reverse cowgirl style, until Kyzer had reached his first orgasm. In the kitchen, Kyzer had lifted Rock 'n Roll Rhonda up onto his kitchen island, and had knocked everything on it to the floor. There, the two of them had sex in the missionary position. In the foyer, Kyzer had lifted her up and held her in the air against the glass wall, and Rock 'n Roll Rhonda had bounced feverishly on his hard dick, until he had reached a second orgasm.

It was a little past midnight when Rock 'n Roll Rhonda and Kyzer made it up to his master bedroom. On top again, Rock 'n Roll Rhonda and Kyzer were kissing, as they both took notice in that how Rock 'n Roll Rhonda was riding him seemed to be more personal.

"Are we fallin' in love?"

"Kyzer, I been in love with you, since I was a little girl."

"Damn."

Chapter Twenty

"So, she's refusing to speak to me? Is she– Why? Tell her– Go tell your mother to get out of that fuckin' truck, and to come talk to me."

"First, don't curse at me."

"You have a fuckin' problem with how I talk?" Victoria asked, glaring at Malcolm Bey's face, then over his shoulder at the SUV his mother refused to get out of. She was feeling insulted by Yasmeen Bey's blatant dismissal of her, and her frustration was almost at its boiling point. "Sweetie, you can do us both a huge favor, and remove yourself from my presence, and replace it with your mother's. I know sign language. You're not needed. Tell her to get out. Now. I don't have all day."

Victoria Beauvais didn't like that she saw no fear in Malcolm Bey's green eyes, as she looked at them. She remembered when he was born. She had given birth to her oldest son, Sab, a month before his mother had given birth to him. Her and Malcolm Bey's mother had frequented the same social circles, and were once pretty close, before the kidnapping of her ex-husband had blown up in her face.

"I'm my mother's ears. I'm my mother's voice. Whatever you gotta say, say it to me, and I'll walk over there and say it to her. Then, I'll come back, and I'll give you her response."

"Fuck this. Move."

Victoria gave Malcolm Bey a look of shock when he grabbed her by the arm when she moved to walk around him. While yanking her arm free, she turned to look at her bodyguards. The twin Russian brothers quickly unholstered their weapons, unconcerned with the fact that they were in the middle of Walmart's huge parking lot on an early Tuesday morning, and dozens of witnesses were around.

"Touch me again."

"I don't have to. You got the point I was tryna make when I did the first time. Ain't nobody gettin' close to my mom, Victoria."

"Fine by me," Victoria snapped, intrigued by Malcolm's calmness, and how unintimidated he seemed to be with her bodyguards. After a quick moment of consideration, she let out a sigh, and looked Malcolm Bey in his eyes. "Your mother and I share a common enemy. It's fine, if she wants to dismiss the past, and our history as friends. I'm okay with that."

"Who's the common enemy?"

"Rock 'n Roll Rhonda. Tia's cousin."

"This about what 'chu did to they uncle?"

"Does that matter?"

"Tia was my sister, Victoria. You know that."

"Tuna wasn't your uncle. Rock 'n Roll Rhonda isn't your cousin."

Victoria watched Malcolm Bey closely. His eyes had drifted out to Columbus Boulevard for a moment. He appeared to be thinking about their discussion, so she remained quiet.

"My mom said that was your son they found dead in that house up North. Rock 'n Roll Rhonda did that?"

"Possibly. He tried to kill me with her a few weeks ago. Maybe, she tied up a loose end, by getting him out of the way. Malcolm, I don't want revenge for my son, if she did do it. His death means nothing to me. It's his father's money I'm after. Rock 'n Roll Rhonda interfered in me finding out where my other son's girlfriend lives. As a favor to your mother, I want to hand deliver Rock 'n Roll Rhonda to her. I'm in possession of something she'll come anywhere for?"

"And what's that?"

"Follow me."

Victoria spun around on her three inch, marble blue, Yves Saint Laurent stilettos, and headed to the rear of her black, 2013 GMC, Denali. Her head nod signaled that she wanted one of her bodyguards to open the rear door for her.

Malcolm Bey eyed the Russian twins cautiously as he followed Victoria's lead. The rear passenger window of the Range Rover Evoque him and his mother had arrived in came down, and his mother's face appeared. It went unseen, but Yasmeen Bey had her hand-Uzi ready, and was preparing to rush to her son's aid, if it was necessary. She hadn't trusted Victoria Beauvais, since she had heard about Victoria Beauvais having an affair with her father's hitman, Craig Barnes. The news of her having her ex-husband kidnapped had only added to her distrust.

There was an immediate rage, and a sense of overprotection in Malcolm Bey's eyes, at the sight of the sleeping toddler in the car seat, as he looked into the backseat of Victoria Beauvais' SUV. The little boy was the son of his deceased, half-sister. He hadn't seen him since her funeral.

Victoria was ignorant to the silent command Malcolm Bey was giving when he took off his baseball hat, ran his hand through his long dreadlocks, then replaced his hat.

The doors on several cars and trucks, parked all in close proximity to where him and Victoria had met, suddenly came open. Victoria's two bodyguards were first to recognize the ambush. They sandwiched Victoria quickly, putting their backs to her, and joining both of their hands to their guns.

"What the fuck you crazy? That's my fuckin' nephew."

"He's my bargaining chip," Victoria argued, counting the addition of men on the scene, and the guns in their hands. Her and her bodyguards were inside their circle, outgunned, and definitely outnumbered. " Malcolm, don't fuckin' touch him. If you do, it'll be a war, between your mother and me."

"We can get that over and done with right now. Shoot first."

Victoria halted the twins when their arms came up to raise their guns, as Malcolm Bey unfastened the seatbelt in their SUV that was securing his nephew's car seat in the backseat. His green eyes burned into hers, once he had his sleeping nephew out of the SUV, and down at his side. Arrogantly, he turned and began to walk away, not once looking over his shoulder at her. Victoria stared past him at his mother, who was watching the dramatic scene unfold.

"This ain't over, Malcolm! Tell that bitch that!"

10:17 a.m.

Endings.

Rock 'n Roll Rhonda stared out of the window down at the busy intersection of 21st and Passyunk. She was anxiously awaiting the phone call from Victoria Beauvais, and for her little cousin's sake, nervously checking the time, every few minutes. She had been up, since the rise of the sun. Her busy night with Kyzer had all of her female parts feeling sore and sensitive.

After checking the time again, Rock 'n Roll Rhonda walked back over to the office desk, and sat in the comfortable chair behind it. She checked the time again and sighed upon seeing that only one minute had gone by, since she had last looked at her cell phone.

"I'm about to call this bitch," Rock 'n Roll Rhonda considered, looking at the cell phone Victoria Beauvais had left with her cousin, Zainab. She touched the screen of the cell phone, brought up the call log, then stared at the only number on the list. "I gotta get Sooly back. This bitch—"

Rock 'n Roll Rhonda hopped up out of the chair and stood when Yasmeen Bey's office door came swinging open. Not wasting a second, she started firing her Glock. The silencer on the gun kept the gunshots muffled. Yasmeen Bey and the person behind her fell backwards, and Rock 'n Roll Rhonda didn't stop shooting at them, until their bodies slammed into the wall out in the daycare center's hallway, and they were motionless down on the floor.

There was joy in Rock 'n Roll Rhonda's chest as she moved with hurried steps to inspect Yasmeen Bey. Her eyes quickly recognized that the male behind Yasmeen Bey had been her son, but it was the child in his arms, that she had not seen, that gave her a feeling that she had only felt once in her life; when she had awakened, to discover that she had mistakenly smothered her three-month-old daughter, while they had been asleep. Rock 'n Roll Rhonda's legs turned into jelly, and she fell to the floor, as she stared horrified at her little cousin's lifeless body. There was blood spilling from the back of his head. His tiny hand was still holding a lollipop.

As Rock 'n Roll Rhonda drove away from Yasmeen Bey's South Philadelphia daycare center, she sobbed uncontrollably, nearly crashing twice. At the intersection of 20th and Bainbridge, she pulled over into an empty parking space, haunted immensely by the grave mistake she had made. Almost at a point of vomiting and hyperventilating, she grudgingly answered her cell phone when it began to ring.

"H–Hello?"

"Girl, I love you so much!! Rhonda, we got him back! We got Sooly back! That bitch tried to get Yasmeen Bey on her side, totally forgettin' the fact that Malcolm was Sooly's uncle! She ain't call you, yet, did she?! Rhonda, Malcolm wanna talk to you about his mom. Look, I know it's a lot."

"Zay?"

"Yes, my favorite cousin? Oh, my God. I can't wait to see him."

"I'm sorry, Zay."

"For what? Are you cryin'? What's wrong? Rhonda?"

Rock 'n Roll Rhonda ended the phone call and dropped her cell phone down to her lap. She couldn't bring herself to admit to her cousin what she had just done. It was a horrible secret she would have to die with, and for now, live with.

Chapter Twenty-One

Rock 'n Roll Rhonda was in the Germantown section of Philadelphia, sobbing uncontrollably as she stood in the first rank with the other Muslim women, observing the evening prayer inside of the masjid. The incident at Yasmeen Bey's daycare center had made national news, and the unsolved, triple murder, was still headlining on all of the local news stations.

Rock 'n Roll Rhonda was an absolute mess, and no one close to her knew how to find her. She had destroyed her cell phone. After the prayer was complete, Rock 'n Roll Rhonda left the masjid quickly. A concerned Muslim woman followed her outside, and around the corner to her parked car.

"As Salaamu Alaykum."

"Wa Laykum As Salaam Wa Rahmatullah," Rock 'n Roll Rhonda responded, opening the driver's side door to her Acura SUV. She saw the empathy and genuine concern in the woman's eyes, but she was in no mood to talk. "Is everything okay?"

"Na'am, na'am. I'm fine. Sister, are you?"

Rock 'n Roll Rhonda sat down and swung her feet inside of her SUV, but left her driver's side door ajar. She was given a moment to compose herself when the young

Muslim woman's cell phone began to ring. She pushed the ignition button to start her SUV, then sat up some, to readjust her Kevlar dress beneath the backs of her thighs. The young Muslim woman kept giving her glances, as she continued to talk on her cell phone, seemingly to apologize for the delay. Once she was done talking, she smiled apologetically, and put her cell phone away.

"That was my husband. We just moved back here from Yemen, and he was just worried, since I wasn't out front, waitin' for him, after the prayer was over. I told him I was around the corner."

"What's your name?"

"Gabrielle. Well, my attribute is Hasanah. That's what I go by."

"I appreciate your concern, but I'm okay now. Shukran."

Rock 'n Roll Rhonda glanced up at her rearview mirror when the young Muslim woman raised her hand, and flagged down a slow driving, white, Audi station wagon.

"That's my husband right there. Yeah, I just wanted to make sure you was okay, because you never know what people might be goin' through. You sure you're okay, though?"

"Yeah, the prayer made me feel a whole lot—"

On impulse, Rock 'n Roll Rhonda lost it when she looked at the face of the driver inside of the Audi station wagon. He had no idea who she was, because of her face veil. He was responsible for the death of Zainab's best friend, Bayyinah. His name was Hakeem. Rock 'n Roll Rhonda snatched her gun from under her driver's seat, pushed the Muslim woman who claimed to be his wife aside, and she started shooting at him over the roof of her truck.

After regaining her footing, the young, Muslim woman, pulled out a gun of her own, and shot Rock 'n Roll Rhonda three times in the back. Rock 'n Roll Rhonda's entire body jerked from the impact, and as she went falling down to her knees, she twisted and aimed her Glock 40 at the young Muslim woman's mid-section, and fired three rapid shots. Rock 'n Roll Rhonda sent five more bullets at her falling body, then got back to her feet, and finished shooting at the driver of the Audi station wagon. The pain in her back was intense, but she knew that none of the bullets had penetrated the Kevlar material of her bulletproof dress. She saw Hakeem slump over his steering wheel, and as his car drifted over to a string of parked cars, where it crashed into the rear of an old, Nissan Maxima, she decided to make an escape, before the police cars she heard in the distance arrived.

Rampage.

11:26 p.m.

The Tenth and Thompson housing project had all of Victoria's attention, as her bodyguard, Dimitri found a place to park their SUV. His brother, like Victoria, was also busy watching everything that was going on out in front of the tall housing project. A small crowd of men were standing at the entrance, smoking cigarettes, weed, and on their cell phones, while making drug transactions to a constant line of drug users, that were coming on foot, or pulling up in cars.

Victoria made a phone call that was brief, then returned her cell phone back to her pocketbook. There was a body warrant out for her arrest, and she was pissed. Someone from Malcolm Bey's click had informed the authorities of their standoff in the parking lot at Walmart, and gave her name as someone with a motive to kill Malcolm Bey, his mother, and his nephew. The thought of it all made her headache throb harder. The death of her ex-husband hadn't caused her this much trouble. Not once did she even think about her youngest son's funeral that had been earlier that morning. Her only concerns were staying out of jail, killing Rock 'n Roll Rhonda, and finding the house where her ex-husband's money was being hidden.

11:32 p.m.

The enemy of my enemy . . .

Is my friend.

"Where'd you get the name Maniac from?"

"Some prosecutor in juvenile court back in the day. After that, it just stuck wit' me."

"Tell me about Rock 'n Roll Rhonda," Victoria requested, as she sat beside Maniac in the backseat of her SUV. Her bodyguards, Dimitri, and Alexie, were standing outside of her door, with their backs to her ""From what I understand, you turned her out. I'm interested in figuring out a solution that can turn her off . . . for good."

Chapter Twenty-Two

Rock 'n Roll Rhonda was sobbing with her face covered by her hands, as she sat with her back against her cousin's marble tombstone. She had been there since the crack of dawn. The cemetery was empty, quiet, and the only place Rock 'n Roll Rhonda wanted to be. Her cousin, Tianna Barnes, had been her role model, and someone she had always aspired to be like.

The horrible mistake she had made, by killing her cousin's son was tormenting Rock 'n Roll Rhonda. She was at her cousin's grave to apologize, but to also decide how to move forward.

Guilt.

Rock 'n Roll Rhonda was physically drained, and emotionally exhausted. She had bags beneath her eyes from a lack of sleep, and the entire left side of her back was bruised and sore. The impact of the three bullets to the Kevlar had caused the bones and muscles in her back to become swollen and ache with stiffness. She had the slightest idea, if Hakeem and his wife had survived or not, nor did she even care. The unexpected confrontation with Hakeem was a drop in a bucket of water, compared to her accidental killing of her little cousin. She believed that she was owed all the pain she was experiencing, but what was stabbing at her heart in all of her agonizing moments, was what she knew her cousin, Zainab, was dealing with, at the loss of their little cousin.

It was an uncomfortable wind continuously passing its way through the Southwest Philadelphia cemetery. The early morning sky was patchy with clouds above it; and in a few hours, there would be dozens of grieving family members a few feet from where Rock 'n Roll Rhonda was crying, to lay her little cousin to rest beside his mother.

With no cell phone, and no contact with anyone, Rock 'n Roll Rhonda was unaware that Victoria Beauvais had been named a person of interest in her little cousin's death. She had been unreachable for three days. She hadn't eaten or showered in two.

Through crying eyes, Rock 'n Roll Rhonda spotted Kyzer's car as it entered the cemetery, and slowly followed the long gravel road. She considered running to her SUV and pulling off, before he reached her, but the pathetic idea came and went. She pulled her knees up to her chest when Kyzer's car momentarily disappeared, as he drove around the area of the cemetery, where there were several mausoleums in place. In that fraction of time, she considered leaving again.

Moments later, Kyzer was pulling up and parking in front of her truck. As he approached, she couldn't meet his stare. Shame wouldn't allow her to. After kneeling down beside her, Kyzer reached out and lifted her face veil. Her eyes started pouring tears.

"Kyzer, I messed up."

"That don't mean you supposed to disappear, Rock 'n Roll. Come on, man. I been everywhere, lookin' for you."

"How you know I was here?"

"I didn't. I woke up this mornin', and I added here to all the places I ain't check on Tuesday, Wednesday, and Thursday. Where the fuck you been at?"

"Hotels."

"Instead of just callin' me? I thought we was in this war together? What changed?"

"Me."

Chapter Twenty-Three

For the entire second weekend of March, Rock 'n Roll Rhonda and Kyzer had stayed inside of Kyzer's house together, and had avoided all contact with the outside world. Every night, except for Sunday, Rock 'n Roll Rhonda had awakened from a deep sleep, crying and screaming. The secret of her accidentally killing her little cousin was acting like poison inside of her soul.

In the early, Sunday morning hours, Kyzer was sitting up in bed when Rock 'n Roll Rhonda returned from the bathroom. Their sense of trust in each other had grown tremendously.

"You alright?"

"My period late," Rock 'n Roll Rhonda admitted, as she climbed back into bed. She kept her eyes on Kyzer's, in an attempt to see his reaction to what she had just revealed, but his expression was unreadable, and the darkness of his bedroom wasn't helping any. "It was supposed to come on Friday."

"You want me to go out and get 'chu a pregnancy test?"

"Maybe, it'll come on tomorrow."

"And what if it don't?"

Rock 'n Roll Rhonda exhaled a long sigh as she laid down. Her and Kyzer had no official title on their relationship, and the idea of her possibly being pregnant with his child had suddenly added a seriousness to how their lives were connected, that hadn't existed before this moment. This new problem, as she thought about it, before walking out of the bathroom, was only another unwanted layer of stress to her life, that she didn't think she could deal with, without losing pieces of her sanity in the process. Everyone believed that Victoria Beauvais was responsible for her little cousin's murder, and Kyzer, and her cousin, Zainab, both assumed that her dark behavior in how she was grieving, was a result of her feeling guilty in not getting her little cousin back like she had promised.

"Kyzer, I wanna finish my list."

"Give it to me. I'll–"

"No, Kyzer. No. Just help me. Tomorrow is Monday. Help me finish that list, then we'll get the pregnancy test at the end of the week."

"Stay right here."

"Why? Kyzer, where you goin'?"

"To one of them twenty-four hour CVS' to get a pregnancy test. I wear the pants. And if you is pregnant, once we done that list, you done wit' all 'lat crazy shit."

"Said the person who knee-deep in crazy shit."

"I can chill."

"How much you wanna bet?"

"Let's bet Maniac. Whoever put him down first, that's who plan we gon' go wit'."

"Count me in."

Chapter Twenty-Four

Monday.
11:56 a.m.
Rock 'n Roll Rhonda knocked on the door several times, then used the gloved-index finger on that same hand to cover the peephole, as she unholstered the gun from her waist with her right hand. She was disguised as a police woman, and wearing Aviator sunglasses. As she stood there, waiting for someone to come to the door, she shot a glance over her shoulder at the owner of the home's parked car.

The woman on the other side of the door opened it, but only to the extent that the security chain would allow. Before the woman could get one single word out of her mouth, Rock 'n Roll Rhonda had her Glock aimed at the woman's face. The horror in the woman's eyes mirrored off of Rock 'n Roll Rhonda's sunglasses, as the first bullet ripped into her mouth, and a second and third one, soon followed. The three gunshots echoed inside of the house, and Rock 'n Roll Rhonda didn't stand there to watch the woman fall.

Calmly, Rock 'n Roll Rhonda turned, walked down the steps, and down Frankford Avenue, until she reached Thompson Street. She walked the entire way with her head down, and she didn't remove her police hat until after

Kyzer had pulled away from the curb, and had made a U-turn. The woman she had killed was Storm's mother.

Rock 'n Roll Rhonda was sure that Storm was responsible for Party's death. She had no idea where Storm might be, but she knew that Storm would come from under whatever rock she was using to hide under, once she learned that her mother had been murdered. Kyzer had advised her to use the tactic. Now she just had to be patient and wait to hear when Storm's mother's funeral would be.

Ties.

That.

Bind.

5:23 p.m.

Rock 'n Roll Rhonda was circling the bound and gagged woman. Her indecisiveness, and sudden loss of desire to kill the crying woman, was purely due to the promise she had made to the woman, a week and a half earlier. As the woman's eyes gave her unheard pleas, each time she walked in front of her, Rock 'n Roll Rhonda reminded herself why the woman had to die, and rationalized why the integrity of her promise to the woman deserved to be undone.

Rock 'n Roll Rhonda circled the woman once more, then stopped in front of her, and removed the gag from her mouth.

"I didn't say anything. I swear, I didn't!"

"You gettin' too loud," Rock 'n Roll Rhonda warned, impulsively pointing her gun at the woman's head to silence her. Because of the woman, she had been given a copy of the keys to Yasmeen Bey's office last week. "Raise your voice again. On the news, they said it wasn't no forced entry, and that the person more than likely got in with a key, or was let in. If they ain't already, all her employees, your ass being one of them, is on the detective's fuckin' suspect list."

"But, listen– Please, just listen to me. Just for one second, okay? My son father dead, and his family don't help me with shit. All this furniture from Rent-A-Center. I'm all my kids have. All they ever—"

Rock 'n Roll Rhonda pointed her gun at the woman's forehead and pulled the trigger. The speed of the bullet snapped the woman's head back violently, and sent her body toppling over backwards in the chair she was bound to. A pool of dark blood immediately began to grow around the woman's face. A moment of guilt paralyzed Rock 'n Roll Rhonda, as her eyes rested on a family picture of the woman and her three young sons, while she walked through the woman's kitchen, and out of the back door.

By far, the murder was the toughest that Rock 'n Roll Rhonda had ever intentionally committed. However, her remorse was being outweighed by all of the critical information Yasmeen Bey's employee had known about her, and what kind of damage that could have on her life. It had been a decision based solely on self-preservation, and selfishness, and at no point of her climbing the fence in the dead woman's backyard, did Rock 'n Roll Rhonda wish she could retrace her steps, and take back what she had done. In the sensitive recesses of her conscious, she was only holding that wish for her little cousin.

Rock 'n Roll Rhonda was indeed pregnant, and with this now being an unexpected, and new dynamic in her life, she was internally feeling scared and concerned for the future of her unborn child. The desperation to stay alive, and remain a free woman, had stealthily mixed into the fabric of her soul as she had slept the prior night.

Still disguised as a police officer, Rock 'n Roll Rhonda turned the corner of 27th and Dickinson, and crossed the street. Her brown eyes were watery, but alert. If a real police officer was to suddenly appear on the scene, she was going to send every illegal bullet in her gun in their direction; Kyzer was too.

Her plans were his.

His plans were hers.

Nobody was better.

10:35 p.m.

Rock 'n Roll Rhonda gave the two bouncers at the front door of the nightclub a mean stare, and they both parted, so her and Kyzer could walk through the front door. The loud music was almost deafening inside of the nightclub. There was barely room to move, and if not for the periodical ceiling lights flashing, and countless club goers being on their cell phones, constantly taking pictures, talking, and on social media, darkness would be prevailing. There was standing-room only inside of the popular, Old City nightclub, and Rock 'n Roll Rhonda and Kyzer were threading their way through the crowd like a hot needle. Her and Kyzer were no longer disguised as cops, and were now dressed as detectives, complete with wigs, reading glasses, fake badges and black suits.

Rock 'n Roll Rhonda led the way into the chaotic dressing room, used by the nightclub's female, exotic dancers. Their unannounced intrusion quickly earned her and Kyzer frowns, angry stares, and nasty comments.

"Jessica Scott, and Regina Anderson!" Rock 'n Roll Rhonda announced, raising her fake badge in the air. All of the half-naked strippers, who weren't the two women whose names she had announced, shot concerned looks at the two women, who the names belonged to, and she followed their stares. "I'm Detective Madison, and this is my partner, Detective Jones. If you're not Jessica or Regina, give us some privacy. Thank you. You'll have your dressing room back in five minutes."

After all of the strippers were out of the dressing room, Kyzer put his back to the door, and crossed his arms over his chest. His eyes went around the dressing room with one fleeting glance. The walls were mirrors, some having pictures taped to them. There was a line of stand-up lockers on both sides of the rear back walls, where there was a door. The floor was littered with high heel shoes of all colors, and sizes, and vibrant colored costumes, made of silk, fishnet, and spandex, were all over the place. The outlets were all occupied with cell phone chargers, and pocketbooks, duffel bags, and carry-on luggage, were on the tables, countertops, and pushed against the lockers and walls.

Jessica Scott, who went by the stripper name, Jesse Minaj, was Puerto Rican, blonde, and beautiful. Both of her arms, and her left ribcage, were covered in colorful tattoos. She was giving Rock 'n Roll Rhonda an impatient stare, while lighting up a cigarette.

Regina Anderson, known around the nightclub as Juicy, hadn't regarded Rock 'n Roll Rhonda, or Kyzer, one time. She was still staring at her half-naked reflection in the mirror, while she applied black, duct tape to one nipple, then the other. She was completely naked, and her body was voluptuous and thick. Without the six-inch, black, stilettos she had on her feet, her natural height was 5'7" tall. Her skin complexion was dark chocolate, and there was confidence and sex appeal, in how she was standing, and the way she was eyeing her own reflection.

"Last month, you two were down Atlanta," Rock 'n Roll Rhonda reminded both strippers, while removing her new cell phone from the inside pocket of her suit jacket. Mentioning Atlanta got a noticeable reaction out of Juicy, and as the stripper's reflection held her stare, she revealed her bombshell, as she held up her cell phone for both Juicy, and Jesse Minaj, to see. "While y'all were down there, y'all posted a cute picture of Honey Myers. The picture was posted on both of y'all Instagram pages. Now, I don't have to remind either one of you, that Honey Myers is a fugitive, and she's wanted for the kidnapping, and murder of Brittany Sim–"

Rock 'n Roll Rhonda stopped talking, and gave the dressing room door an angry look. Someone on the opposite side of the closed door had started knocking on it incessantly. Kyzer and Rock 'n Roll Rhonda both got the shocks of their lives, after Kyzer snatched the dressing room door open. Detective Konn was standing there with his badge in the air, and his gun drawn. The smile on his face was ugly, and arrogant, until Kyzer grabbed him by the collar and yanked him into the dressing room, and Rock 'n Roll Rhonda hit a light switch, bringing total darkness to the dressing room.

Instant madness ensued inside of the dark dressing room. The two strippers dove to the floor, and went hiding for cover. Kyzer and Detective Konn were wrestling for control of the other's gun hand, crashing against the walls, twisting, turning, kneeing, elbowing, and shooting. Each time one of the strippers screamed, Rock 'n Roll Rhonda was sending bullets in that direction.

The illumination of the three muzzle flashes provided brief glimpses of the enemy ensemble, fighting for their lives inside of the dressing room. The silence of the guns was followed by a lot of heavy breathing, coming from only two people.

Kyzer kept his eyes down and his head low, as Rock 'n Roll Rhonda led him by the hand through the crowded nightclub. His appearance was in disarray. He had lost his glasses in the fight with Detective Konn, and his fake beard was hanging loosely from the left side of his face. People were giving him strange looks as he passed them. He had never been inside of the popular nightclub before, and had only heard stories about it. His deceased girlfriend, was once the manager of the nightclub, until one of the strippers had participated in her kidnapping, and later, her ultimate death.

Rock 'n Roll Rhonda could feel her heart beating a mile a minute, as she led Kyzer through the crowded hallway of the nightclub. She knew the building like the back of her hand, and knew where all of the surveillance cameras were located. Still, she knew that by now, the small massacre Kyzer and her had left behind in the dressing room had been discovered. Earlier that morning, her and Kyzer had visited the nightclub's DJ, and had paid him twenty-five thousand dollars to keep the music loud, once he had seen them entering the dressing room. Detective Konn's unexpected appearance had forced them to use more gunshots than they had both intended.

At the rear door, which was only used by staff, a tall, Puerto Rican bouncer, built like a football player, handed Rock 'n Roll Rhonda the hard-drive of a computer, and he gave Kyzer a handful of flash-drives, as he pushed the rear door open for them. The cool night breeze swept into the nightclub from the nightclub's parking lot, and Rock 'n Roll Rhonda and Kyzer went in opposite directions, the moment they stepped foot outside.

Tandem.

2:14 a.m.

As Kyzer slept in bed beside her, Rock 'n Roll Rhonda was wide awake, sometimes staring across the bedroom at the huge flat-screen TV on the wall, and sometimes, she would use her new cell phone to log onto social media, and sit there silently, monitoring what was going on. She had created a fake Facebook and Instagram account, and with them, she was viewing all of the comments being made by everyone that had been at the nightclub, Gossip Alley, earlier tonight. Detective Konn and both of the strippers had died at nearby hospitals from their gunshot wounds. There was a huge outpouring of support on the nightclub's Instagram page for both strippers. Detective Konn received none.

The Facebook pages of all of the local news stations in Philadelphia had lengthy segments on each incident that

Rock 'n Roll Rhonda had been involved in. According to the authorities, there were no motives they knew of, and they had no suspects, except for the witnesses accounts of the two detectives that had come into the dressing room at the nightclub, requesting to only speak to Regina Anderson, and Jessica Scott. Their descriptions of the detectives were what Rock 'n Roll Rhonda and Kyzer had hoped for. It was Detective Konn's surprising arrival that had Rock 'n Roll Rhonda still feeling unnerved.

"Kyzer?"

Kyzer blinked his eyes open, then rolled over and faced Rock 'n Roll Rhonda. After setting her cell phone on the nightstand, and using the remote control to cut off the TV, she laid down and snuggled up close to Kyzer's chest. He had closed his eyes again, and wrapped an arm over her shoulder.

"Kyzer?"

"Yo?"

"You ever kill somebody you ain't want to?"

"Umm-hmm."

"Who?"

Rock 'n Roll Rhonda watched as Kyzer blinked his eyes open and looked into hers. He sighed and stayed silent so long, while holding her stare, she began to wonder if he would give her an answer.

Kyzer was peculiar in a way that Rock 'n Roll Rhonda found endearing. He thought a lot. His seriousness was also well balanced with his humor, and most of all, in his company she felt safe, happy, and eager to learn everything that he was willing to share with her. Being pregnant with his child had her more afraid of death and jail, than she had ever been, since she had turned to a life of crime and rebelliousness. In all of her past relationships, her boyfriends had always been a lot calmer than she was. None of them had been into the streets. This dynamic had always given her reasons to feel content that, if she had a child with any of them, and something untimely happened to her, her child would still have a parent to look after them. Because Kyzer was as wild and unpredictable as her, and after their close call with Detective Konn earlier tonight, Rock 'n Roll Rhonda was afraid of the unlikely, and the unknown.

Anxieties.

"I ain't wanna do my first hit. My oldhead, Manny Yunk, came and got me one day. This dude he knew from some upstate jail had got back in court, and got a new trial. They was offerin' him a fifteen to thirty. He ain't want it, though. I think he had like twelve in. He wanted to come home with no parole. So, his obstacle was this one witness. If the witness was out the way, the case was gon' go away. He gave Manny Yunk ten stacks to find somebody to do it."

"Who was the witness?"

"His dad."

Chapter Twenty-Five

Tuesday.

9:35 p.m.

"I didn't do that, Salvatore. I swear to you, I didn't."

"Then, tell me who did?"

Victoria held Salvatore Masino's stare, until he looked away. The tone of voice he had used with her had been a clear indication that her presence no longer intimidated him as it once did in the past. He obviously still held a great deal of respect for her, but she was sensing that his fear of her had dwindled tremendously.

As the two of them sat across from one another at their restaurant table, pretending to be a couple, the tension between both of them was thick, and palpable.

The upscale restaurant was located just off a main highway in Atlantic City, New Jersey. Salvatore Masino was a close friend of the restaurant's owner. Victoria knew the owner as well. His name was Patrick O'Malley. He was Irish, in his late sixties, and until a recent secret indictment, he had been one of the biggest prescription pill suppliers in Atlantic City. It was unknown to Victoria and Salvatore Masino, but their longtime friend, Patrick O'Malley, was now a federal informant, and there was a recording device hidden discreetly beneath their secluded restaurant table.

"Salvatore, I was using the kid for leverage," Victoria explained, after lifting her glass of red wine to her lips and taking a sip. She glanced over at her bodyguards, who were both sitting at the restaurant's bar, taking advantage of the permission she had given them to drink as much as they wanted. "I never planned on hurting him. He was safe, while he was with me, Salvatore. The only kids I ever wanted to kill, were my fuckin' own. Tia's cousins loved that little boy, and wouldn't've thought once about shooting at me, while I had him. I want 'chu to think about that. Yasmeen's son intervened. Now, if you asked me, I think that little bitch, Rock 'n Roll Rhonda, made a huge mistake, Sal. I think she was there to kill Yasmeen, and she didn't realize her little cousin—"

"Impossible."

"Is it?"

"Of course. From everything I've heard about her, that kind of mistake—Victoria, I'm not accepting that story. I won't. The kid's father will be home soon. You and whoever was responsible for his death will face that storm when he does. That detective that was murdered with them strippers at his club was the only real problem for me and him. My nephew has no more legs to stand on. This thing with Rock 'n Roll Rhonda . . . squash it."

"That suggestion sounds odd, coming from you."

"Just take some advice from an old friend. Squash it."

"You were the same old friend, who gave me an STD, I accused my husband of having."

"And I apologized, didn't I? Geez, what do you want from me?"

Victoria glared across the restaurant table at Salvatore Masino, while tapping her manicured fingernails on her glass of wine. During her affair with him, she had enjoyed some of the best sex she had ever experienced. His oral sex on her was still hard to get out of her mind. Victoria raised her wine glass to her lips and took a generous sip. She wanted to erupt in laughter, because decades earlier, she had the opinion that Salvatore Masino reminded her so much of the Fonz, and now, as she looked across the restaurant table at the ageing, Italian man, she was reminded of an out of shape, and tanned, Bernie Sanders, who had way too much black dye in his balding hair.

"So, who do you need these two keys of coke for, Victoria?"

"A new acquaintance of mine."

"Really? Young or old?"

"Is these the questions you ask everyone you do business with?"

"Well, if my memory serves me correctly, you wanted this to be a favor. Isn't that what you called it?"

"Favor, or not, are all these questions necessary?"

"They are."

"Forget it, Sal," Victoria snapped, pushing her chair away from the restaurant table. She rose to her feet, then grabbed her clutch purse from the table. "You prick. You're nothing without Carmen and Trixie. All that fuckin' money Pierre made for you, it was because of me. Me, Sal. A million fuckin' questions about two keys? That's how you're going to treat me? You, Splash, Rock 'n Roll Rhonda, and anyone else you can name, better watch y'all back."

"Victoria, relax. Sit down. Stop with the–"

"Kiss my ass, Sal."

"Victoria, I'll do it."

Victoria stood there. Her grey eyes were ablaze, and her chest was rising and falling, as she stared angry daggers at Salvatore Masino. The hand that was holding her purse was shaking against her hip.

"Victoria, sit back down."

"Hell no."

"Well, we do need to discuss where and when I'll be getting those two keys to you, right? Let's finish this wine."

"You have my number. Call me when you're ready."

"What about the wine?"

For a long moment, Victoria continued to stare angrily at Salvatore Masino. Her bodyguards had been giving her a watchful eye, since she had risen to her feet. Pointing her index finger threateningly at Salvatore Masino, Victoria grabbed their half empty wine bottle from their restaurant table and stormed off. Salvatore Masino watched as her bodyguards hurried after her. The moment Victoria and her bodyguards were out of the restaurant, he sent a text-message to Rock 'n Roll Rhonda.

Chapter Twenty-Six

Wednesday.
3:50 p.m.

Rock 'n Roll Rhonda and her cousin, Zainab, were fighting like they were strangers, and one didn't know the other. The rage between the cousins was boiling and uncontrollable, and as they were both punching and scratching, Rock 'n Roll Rhonda's gun fell to the pavement.

Zainab's grandmother came hurrying from behind her screen door, and down her front steps at the sight of Rock 'n Roll Rhonda's gun.

"Don't touch my– Ms.Thelma, don't touch my fuckin' gun!"

"Gran'mom, get it!"

Rock 'n Roll Rhonda and her cousin were both dressed in black, overgarments, and were wearing face-veils. With a firm grip on the black fabric of her cousin's headscarf, Rock 'n Roll Rhonda kept swinging wildly at her cousin's face, while she began to push her backwards. Neighbors on both sides of York Street were on their steps, and watching the family dispute. A female teenager was in a bedroom window, recording the fight with her cell phone two houses away.

Zainab's grandmother buckled when Rock 'n Roll Rhonda shoved Zainab into her. Zainab lost her footing, after stepping on the long fabric of her overgarment, and her weight sent her grandmother falling hard to the ground.

In one step, Rock 'n Roll Rhonda had her gun in her hand, and was standing over Zainab, and Zainab's grandmother.

"Rhonda, I fuckin' wish you would. You got that kimar, that niqab, and that hijab on, but I know who you are underneath. If you wasn't on the run, you wouldn't even be covered. You killed Sooly. That's why you been avoidin' me."

Rock 'n Roll Rhonda backed away, then turned, and began to walk with fast steps.

"And when that bitch, Victoria, kill you, I'm gon' make sure none of the masjids accept your body for your janazah!"

The threat brought a rush of tears to Rock 'n Roll Rhonda's eyes and made her run, as she turned the corner of 3rd and York. Her tears were blinding her eyes, and she could barely see. Crossing 3rd Street, a sob caught in her throat as she climbed into her rental car. Her cousin's words had been critical, and profoundly damaging. She sped away from the curb, crying and overwhelmed with guilt and shame.

Shunned.

6:21 p.m.

There was a billboard on the I-95 expressway with a gigantic picture of Rock 'n Roll Rhonda's face. She was on the Philly's 'Most Wanted' list, and in the past two days, they had shown her picture on the news on both mornings, both afternoons, and one evening. Detectives had recovered some grainy, surveillance footage, from a neighbor's house, showing her walking down Frankford Avenue from Storm's mother's house. The police were asking for help from anyone that might recognize the woman, who had impersonated being a police officer.

The fight with her cousin, and these things, were all on Rock 'n Roll Rhonda's mind, as she sat in Party's barber shop, talking to his sister-in-law, Sabreena.

"Their uncle is taking it real hard. Party wanted to come back to Philly so bad. He used to complain how Boston was boring, and there was nothing for him to really do there."

"Who was the girl with him?"

"Camille."

"They said she worked here."

"She did. She was our shampoo girl."

"Did you tell his brother that Storm did it?"

"I told him everything you told me. I went to see him Saturday."

Rock 'n Roll Rhonda looked around the barber shop, remembering Party. She had only known him for two weeks, but he had been easy to grow fond of. His young heart had impressed her. She would never forget the day he had joined her in shooting at his mother on the I-95 expressway, and their run-in with the off-duty cop.

"Do you believe all the stories people say about Victoria?"

"Which ones? There's a lot of them."

"About her lipstick and perfume."

"It's truth to them."

"With my uncle, we just thought he was over white women. I can't think of one black, or Puerto Rican, woman, for that matter, that he ever messed with, until Victoria."

"I had a twin brother."

"You?"

"Yup. Identical. Two minutes apart. Victoria had him under her spell, and none of us knew it. He helped her kidnap Party and Sab's dad. And, um, it all came out. Sab killed him right in front of me. It's a secret I've been keepin' from my parents for years."

Rock 'n Roll Rhonda watched Sabreena as she dealt with the uncomfortable emotions her memory had brought back to the surface.

"You wanna be there when I kill her?"

"I wanna be there to help. I owe her that much."

"If Salvatore can put her in that position for us, we'll both have our moment."

Avalanches.

8:15 p.m.

The skies above Philadelphia were dark, and the moon was bright and full. The quiet, Wednesday evening, was suddenly disturbed by the intimidating sound of loud gunshots in the Ludlow section of North Philadelphia.

At a red light, Rock 'n Roll Rhonda had flipped up her face veil to examine the cut beneath her left eye, from her fight with her cousin, Zainab. It wasn't that she had underestimated the person behind the wheel of the newer model, silver, Lincoln MKZ. She had only lowered her guard, because the woman in the Lincoln at the red light, waiting beside her was also Muslim, but mostly because there were small children inside of the vehicle with the Muslim woman.

Rock 'n Roll Rhonda leaned to her right as her rental car's driver's side window exploded, and the glass flew over her head and shoulders. Using her right hand, she yanked her steering wheel to her right, and slammed her foot on the gas pedal. The Chevy Impala bolted forward and went up on the curb, and into the traffic light. Rock 'n Roll Rhonda hadn't been wearing a seatbelt, so after her body slammed into the steering wheel, and the air-bag was deployed, she took a moment to grab her pocketbook, while climbing over to the passenger seat. She escaped from the car on her hands and knees through the passenger door, and she stumbled to her feet, pulling her gun from her pocketbook.

The Muslim woman ran out into the middle of the 6th and Master intersection, still shooting at Rock 'n Roll Rhonda.

"I'm Hasaan sister, bitch! I'm Jamillah!!"

Out of her peripheral vision, Rock 'n Roll Rhonda could see the small children inside of the Lincoln MKZ with their crying faces pressed against the windows. Rock 'n Roll Rhonda, even in her feeling justified to return fire, chose to retreat. There was no way she could fire her gun in the direction of the children, and live with herself. What she had done to her little cousin wouldn't allow her to even consider it.

Police sirens were screaming in the night air as she ran west up Master Street. The Muslim woman was the sister of a man she had killed. She was also a very close friend of Kyzer's. Walking south down Marshall Street, Rock 'n Roll Rhonda pulled out her cell phone and called Kyzer. Her whole body was shaking with a new animosity that felt strange as she listened to the sound of screeching tires peeling off in the far distance behind her. If Kyzer's friend chose to circle the block to confront her again, Rock 'n Roll Rhonda wasn't sure of what her actions would be. One thing she was certain of, the unborn child in her stomach was just as important as anyone else's child, and that feeling as a mother was fueling her contempt as she got closer to Thompson Street.

"Hello?"

"'Hasaan's sister just shot at me, Kyzer."

"Who? Jamillah?"

Rock 'n Roll Rhonda turned west up Thompson Street at the sight of a string of police cars racing the wrong way up 6th Street and Randolph Street. Their sirens were loud and blaring, and on foot, heading in the direction she was walking, she was putting her life in even more danger. It would only take for one person from the Tenth and

Thompson projects to notice her, and depending on who that person was, they were going to call the cops, or call for hitmen. At the moment, she wasn't in any position to deal with any hitmen.

"Kyzer, that bitch shot at me with her kids in the fuckin' car!"

"Well, like, what 'chu expect?! You rocked her brother! Where you at? Just come home. I'll straighten–"

"Who side are you on?!" Rock 'n Roll Rhonda snapped, as she stopped at the corner of 7th and Thompson and placed her back against the wall of the post office. She had been fighting back the urge to scream and yell at Kyzer, but his position of seeming to defend what his friend had just done was too much for her to take. "So, it would've been okay for her to shoot me?! Or kill me?! Is that what I'm hearin' you tell me?! Kyzer, I been tryna apologize to her! Do she know about me and you?!"

"No."

"Am I secret?!"

"Stop hollerin' at me!"

"I asked you a fuckin' question, Kyzer! Am I secret?! Do your friends know about me?!"

Silence.

"Kyzer, you know what?" Rock 'n Roll Rhonda sighed, as tears came to her eyes and she considered the gravity of what her heart was inspiring her to say. As she stood there, alone, she knew her next words would subtract one of the few people she had left in her troubled life. "You wanna be on her side? I'ma help y'all get matchin' tombstones."

"Don't threaten me with a good time. You know where to find me."

Hearts.

Divided.

Chapter Twenty-Seven

Thursday.
11:56 a.m.

"That damn ride felt like it would never end."

"It's just my opinion, but I think, given your current situation, you should always consider gettin' around like that."

"Yeah, but not in them tiny ass cars," Rock 'n Roll Rhonda complained, watching as the Uber driver pulled away from the curb and merged the red, mini-cooper, into the busy, 2nd Street traffic. She stood beside Salvatore Masino, holding a suitcase in each hand, waiting for the traffic to slow down, so they both could cross to the other side of 2nd Street. "And she was doin' too much. On her phone, sendin' fuckin' text-messages. Face-Time. Twitter. Postin' selfies at every damn red light for Instagram. And, like, for who? She look like she was born outta somebody ass."

Rock 'n Roll Rhonda followed Salvatore Masino across 2nd Street, and up to a brown-painted door of a factory, on the Cecil B. Moore Avenue side of its large building. There was a surveillance camera aiming down at them from above the door. Giving the camera nothing more than a glance, Rock 'n Roll Rhonda sat both of her suitcases down on the pavement, and began giving her surroundings some thoughtful observation.

After Salvatore Masino used a key to open the door to the factory, Rock 'n Roll Rhonda grabbed her suitcases and followed him inside. She frowned and covered her mouth and nose at the offensive and strong smell of plastic and gasoline, as Salvatore disappeared to find a light switch.

"It stink in here."

"It does, doesn't it?"

Salvatore Masino's voice echoed around the darkness of the factory, and Rock 'n Roll Rhonda looked in the direction that she had heard movement. The lights in the factory suddenly came on, and Salvatore Masino reappeared from behind a pile of old tires and ladders.

"Okay, let me show you the office. My bodyguards are on their way here to get me. I have a busy day ahead of myself, too."

"I hope it don't smell like this in the office," Rock 'n Roll Rhonda commented, as she followed Salvatore Masino. While walking, she looked around at the interior of the factory. "It's definitely a lot of space in here, like you said. And I don't have to worry about no unexpected visitors, right?"

"Not at all."

"Perfect."

"Just leave it like you found it."

"They won't even know I was here."

"Well, it's all yours, until Saturday."

"Thank you, Salvatore."

"Don't mention it."

Inside of the office, Salvatore Masino turned and took the suitcases from Rock 'n Roll Rhonda's hands, and walked over to a large table against a wall, and placed them both there. He exhaled a heavy sigh, once he was done.

The office had a much better ventilation system, and there was a window behind its office desk that provided a view of 2nd Street. Rock 'n Roll Rhonda parted the blinds and stared out of the window at the 2nd Street traffic, thinking for a moment, before turning around to face Salvatore Masino. He had walked over to the office's doorway, and was standing there. The factory belonged to his friend, Miguel Sanchez, and she was given full use of the factory for three whole days. Its North Philadelphia location was geometrically perfect for the violent ideas she had in mind, and by Saturday, she planned on being done with the hit list she had created.

"You be safe, okay?"

"Salvatore, I really appreciate this," Rock 'n Roll Rhonda spoke, almost becoming choked up with emotions. She sat down on the edge of the office desk, cleared her throat, before continuing to speak. "This really means a lot. When all of this is done, Salvatore, I'm gon' need another favor from you. I have to get outta Philly. I have few people I can trust, and even fewer people that I can trust with my life. Somebody, and I still haven't found out who, turned me in the last time I got locked up. I used different guns on all of those situations, so they can't really connect each crime, or think it's the same person. Salvatore, I'm pregnant, and I'm gon' need to be somewhere, so my baby can be healthy. I need to see a doctor. I wanna leave Sunday, Salvatore."

"If you come out of all of this alive, I'll make sure you're well taken care of. Tia would want me to."

After Salvatore Masino was gone, Rock 'n Roll Rhonda walked over to her two suitcases and unzipped them both. In them, she had guns, extra clips, disguises, phony IDs, stolen license plates, a Kevlar dress, and a hundred and fifty thousand dollars in cash. Rock 'n Roll Rhonda made a call on her cell phone, and held it against her ear, while using her free hand to unpack her suitcases.

"Hello?"

"Bam?"

"What's the deal, Rock 'n Roll? Everything situated?"

"You already know."

"So, where we at wit' it? I got Crakk and Odie wit' me right now. Lil Chris on his way, too."

"Bring everybody to Second and Cecil B. Moore."

"Say less."

Ties.

That.

Bind.

7:38 p.m.

Victoria had never killed someone with a gun, but in a matter of moments, she was about to. She was feeling unsure of herself, and slightly nervous. Her bodyguards could sense her unease. At the age of nine, her twin aunts had forced her to slice the throat of a man twice her age, as they held him down for her in the back of their family store in New Orleans. She had cried, dropping the extremely sharp dagger several times, and had only found the courage to follow through with the act, only because she had wanted her aunts to stop berating her, and stinging her ears with their vile curse words.

All of Victoria's sacrifices of men, women, and animals, had been done with knives. Her killings had all been intimate and in places, where she had been comfortable.

"I'm getting out," Victoria announced, flipping the face-veil down to hide her face, and pushing the rear, passenger door open. The Muslim overgarments she was disguised in made her feel like she was being stifled. "I expect to be able to get right in the truck as soon as I'm done."

Victoria pushed the SUV door closed and started walking south on 5th Street, cutting her grey eyes at her surroundings. She was in the Fairhill section of North Philadelphia, an area she wasn't too familiar with. Sighing, she put her eyes on the woman she intended to murder.

The woman was unpacking groceries from her car, and taking the bags to the front steps of her three-story house. The woman was Muslim, also wearing a black face-veil, and appeared to be agitated about something. There was an infant in a car seat in the backseat of her Lincoln MKZ, and two children in the open doorway of the woman's house. One of them looked up the street at Victoria as she closed the distance between them.

Victoria's bodyguard, Dimitri, pulled away from the curb and steered the black, GMC Denali, up to the intersection of 5th and Dauphin, and made a quick right turn onto Dauphin Street and disappeared. He was circling the block.

A step away from the Muslim woman, Victoria stopped and pulled out her bodyguard's handgun. She didn't raise it, until the Muslim woman turned around to see why her children were suddenly screaming in the doorway. The Muslim woman's eyes looked into hers, instantly radiating fear for her children's safety, and none for herself.

As the Muslim woman's children watched, Victoria shot the Muslim woman several times in the chest, then stood over her and shot her some more, after she had fallen to the ground. The children's screams sent Victoria running out into the middle of 5th Street, and down towards Susquehanna Avenue. Neighbors from both sides of the street came running outside, and then, as her bodyguards appeared at the intersection of 5th and Susquehanna, Victoria seized the opportunity she had been hoping for, as she ran up to her SUV.

"Nobody fucks with Rock 'n Roll Rhonda!! Nobody!!!"

11:25 p.m.

Ready.

Aim.

Fire.

If it was one thing the last few months had taught Rock 'n Roll Rhonda, it was that the street life in Philadelphia had suddenly become unhonorable, and was being ran by an abstract new set of rules, that no longer catered to the men and women of respect. The unthinkable was now occurring, and at an all-time high. More than 75% of the criminals in Philadelphia were either working with the state as a confidential informant, or cooperating with the federal authorities, in and out of prison. Killers with decades-long careers of being stand-up men, were now shocking the streets, by revealing street secrets to authorities to make it back home one day, or to stay out of jail altogether. There were major drug suppliers wearing wires now, double-crossing lower level drug dealers, who were under the excited assumption that they had finally found the drug connection they had long been hoping to meet.

Philadelphia.

Wiretaps.

All day, Rock 'n Roll Rhonda had been contemplating long and hard. Her thinking had become more intense when Kyzer had called her hours earlier from a hospital, where Jamillah, Hasaan's sister, was fighting for her life. The person responsible for shooting Jamillah had claimed to be her.

With a sigh, Rock 'n Roll Rhonda rose from behind the office desk, looking at the time on her cell phone. The atmosphere inside of the factory was alive with violent excitement, and dangerous energy. Under other circumstances, the factory was used by Salvatore Masino's friend, as a drop-off, and pick-up spot, for a Mexican drug cartel. Normally, the factory was full of large amounts of money, heroin, and cocaine, and sometimes, Mexican immigrants. Eighteen-wheelers were always coming and going from the factory at all hours of the day and night. Tonight, there was an ensemble of characters inside of the factory, that, collectively, were responsible for more than fifty, unsolved murders; not including the ones that Rock 'n Roll Rhonda was responsible for.

Rock 'n Roll Rhonda stood in the doorway of the office, watching her friends, as they talked, and finished assembling their guns. The sight of the eight men was a definite boost for her morale.

Bam was at the rear of his black, G-wagon, Mercedes-Benz, on his cell phone, as he smoked a cigarette. He was in his early 20s, Puerto Rican, and covered with tattoos. His older sister had been Rock 'n Roll Rhonda's cellmate at Philadelphia's county prison for women. Him and his sister were both from the Juniata section of Philadelphia, and Bam could be found on M and Lycoming on any day of the week. He had love and loyalty tattooed on his face, two Glock 40s on his waist, and a bulletproof vest on over his T-shirt.

Crakk had arrived in a smoke-gray, Jeep Grand Cherokee SRT8, with his friend, Dev. Both men were from Walnut and Franklin, in Pottstown, Pennsylvania. Crakk had served time with Bam at an upstate prison, and had recently come home. He was tall and slim, and covered with tattoos. Dev was a few inches shorter than Crakk, and was also covered with tattoos. The duo looked young, but their eyes reflected a deadly glare that any wise man would understand to mean that they were both about drama. Crakk and Dev were almost done assembling their SKS assault rifles.

Odie was walking in a circle at the front of the black, Audi A8 he had driven from Norristown in. He was talking on his cell phone, as he held his FN-S7 down at his side. When he noticed that Rock 'n Roll Rhonda was watching him, he gave her a nod. He had arrived with his friends, BP, LR, and Ladda Boi. All four men were wearing bulletproof vests. Like Crakk, Odie had just come home from an upstate prison, after turning over a life sentence on his direct appeal. He was tall, light brown, and slim, and in his early 20s, and had tattooed sleeves on both of his arms. In Norristown, Odie was from Oak and Smith, and if you went against him and his squad, most people didn't live to learn from that fatal mistake.

Lil Chris was the quietest of the eight men, and appeared to be the calmest. He had driven up to the factory from South Philadelphia in a silver, GMC Terrain Denali. The SUV was equipped with bulletproof doors, windows, and tires. Looking at Lil Chris, Rock 'n Roll Rhonda was reminded of Kyzer. He was alone, but his aura carried the momentum of a small army. Lil Chris had a light brown complexion, was of medium height, and had an athletic build. His father had been a legend, and he was walking the same path of one day becoming one himself. He was from 20th and Tasker, and he was in his mid-20s. The loud music from his SUV had everybody in the factory nodding their heads. Eerily, he was playing Rick Ross' song, 'Nobody', featuring French Montana.

Riot.

Squad.

12:19 a.m.

Rock 'n Roll Rhonda had learned so many things from her old mentor, Maniac. She had been taught how to assemble and disassemble almost every gun ever made. She had been advised about which companies produced the best weapons, and which ones were known for their defective products. Maniac had showed her how to cook cocaine, cut it, and bag it. She knew how to spot counterfeit money, when to strike an enemy, and if it was ever desperately necessary, where in Philadelphia, the cops would never consider looking for her. An old boyfriend of Rock 'n Roll Rhonda's had been Maniac's younger cousin. His death had joined their fates, and in Rock 'n Roll Rhonda's moment of grieving, Maniac had manipulated her into becoming a war machine.

Maniac was a handsome man, standing over six feet tall, with wide shoulders, and a muscular build. He was intelligent, and was in control of every housing project in North Philadelphia. A shootout with Kyzer several months earlier had left him with half a leg, and bitter forever.

Tonight, as Rock 'n Roll Rhonda was walking west up Girard Avenue, she was hoping to leave Maniac with half a soul. She had created a fake Instagram account, and had been following his every move for a week. She was using the picture of an Ethiopian princess she had found online, as her profile picture. Maniac and several of his friends had been posting pictures of themselves at a neighborhood bar, located at 7th and Girard. Their decision to go there had surprised Rock 'n Roll Rhonda, because the bar was in Kyzer's territory, and Maniac clearly knew this.

As Rock 'n Roll Rhonda was crossing 6th Street, she heard the sounds of 4-wheelers and dirt bikes, and immediately knew that the window of opportunity she had to kill Maniac had just been put on a timer. She shot a look up 6th Street and the sight of five 4-wheelers racing her way confirmed her suspicions. Rock 'n Roll Rhonda hurried her steps, while purposely turning her face away from the gas station as she passed it. There were surveillance cameras positioned all over the gas station. Rock 'n Roll Rhonda could feel her heart rate increasing, as she pictured the madness that was about to unfold.

The Jungle Boys were on their dirt bikes and 4-wheelers, and Rock 'n Roll Rhonda was sure that Kyzer had sent them to confront Maniac. She was certain that someone inside the bar had notified Kyzer of Maniac's presence.

Lil Chris flashed his high beams on his SUV when Rock 'n Roll Rhonda reached the intersection of Marshall and Girard. He was pulling over and parking on the opposite side of Girard Avenue, on 7th Street, facing north. Crakk, Odie, and Bam, were climbing out. The five 4-wheelers cutting through the gas station snatched their attention. Rock 'n Roll Rhonda stopped, and let the young men on the 4-wheelers pass her. Dev, BP, LR, and Ladda Boi, were on the opposite side of Girard Avenue from Rock 'n Roll Rhonda. The four men had paused when Rock 'n Roll Rhonda did, and like her, were seconds from pulling out their guns, as a group of young men on dirt bikes came speeding out into sight from 7th Street, joining the five 4-wheelers. Seconds later, three more 4-wheelers, and two dirt bikes came racing out into the middle of Girard Avenue from Franklin Street.

The young men on the 4-wheelers and dirt bikes started circling the intersection of 7th and Girard, casting stares at the bar, and in the direction of Lil Chris, Odie, Crakk, and Bam. Rock 'n Roll Rhonda took a deep breath, then pulled her guns from her waist and started throwing bullets at the Jungle Boys. In that same moment, Maniac and fifteen of his friends, men, and women, came rushing out of the bar, also shooting at the Jungle Boys.

The Jungle Boys were experts at riding dirt bikes and 4-wheelers. The moment the shooting began, they started popping wheelies, and pulling out their guns, and returning fire.

A police camera fixed on the pole of a traffic light was recording the entire incident. The shootout grew more intense when Kyzer ran up to the edge of the laundromat's roof on 7th and Girard, and began spraying an assault rifle at Maniac and anyone with him. Kyzer's sudden presence, and where he was, left Rock 'n Roll Rhonda momentarily shocked as she went running at top speed down Marshall street. She had noticed that many of Maniac's friends were fleeing down 7th Street, so she was hoping to cut them off down at Thompson Street.

Rock 'n Roll Rhonda had decided against wearing her overgarments tonight, or her Kevlar dress. She was dressed in a black, Nike sweat suit jacket, some black, Balmain jeans, and she was wearing some black, Dior Homme sneakers on her feet. Her hair was pulled back into a tight ponytail, and she had a black, Nike hat on her head, pulled low to her eyebrows. She was dressed to kill. Down at Marshall and Thompson, Rock 'n Roll Rhonda turned left, raising the gun in her right hand first. None of Maniac's friends had made it down to Thompson Street yet.

Rock 'n Roll Rhonda thought of how far she was away from Lil Chris' SUV, as her left shoulder scraped against the wall of the post office, while running up to 7th Street. She had the Glock in her right hand aiming forward, and the one in her left hand down at her side. The echoes of gunshots and yelling met her when she reached 7th Street and turned the corner. Maniac's friends were running down 7th Street like a stampede. Some were shooting as they fled, and others were running behind parked cars, and using them for shields. Rock 'n Roll Rhonda saw one man drop to the street and hide under one.

Maliciously, Rock 'n Roll Rhonda met the fleeing stampede with both of her guns high, and pumping both Glock triggers. She ran out into the middle of 7th Street, aiming and shooting. When she got to the parked car the man had hid under, she slowly walked around it, shooting out each tire as she passed it. The man's screams were gut wrenching as the vehicle's tires quickly began to lose air, and the car began to crush him beneath it. One by one, Rock 'n Roll Rhonda killed her way back up to Girard Avenue.

The police sirens could be heard, but many of the people involved in the shootout didn't seem to care one bit.

The second Rock 'n Roll Rhonda showed her face back at the shootout, Kyzer started throwing tumbling bullets from his assault rifle at her. He believed she was responsible for his friend, Jamillah's death. Rock 'n Roll

Rhonda took cover behind the wall of the bar, and to show Kyzer that his life was no more important, than hers or their unborn child's was to him, she took a deep breath and started emptying her clips as she ran across Girard Avenue to Lil Chris' bulletproof SUV. Odie, Crakk, and Bam, all ran out to meet her, while shooting up at Kyzer, and the remaining Jungle Boys, who were still racing their 4-wheelers and dirt bikes around them, as they continued to daringly trade bullets.

Police cars could be seen, racing up Girard Avenue from both directions. Their lights were flashing on the roofs of their cars wildly, as they seemingly began to speed up.

Kyzer ducked out of sight, and simultaneously, after another moment of trading bullets, the Jungle Boys also raced away. Maniac was crawling on the pavement a block away. He had been shot by Bam twice in the stomach, and once by one of the Jungle Boys. His orthopedic leg and Gucci sneaker was out in the middle of Girard Avenue.

Rock 'n Roll Rhonda and everyone else started piling into Lil Chris' SUV. Ladda Boi was last to climb in, as Lil Chris sped across Girard Avenue, and up 7th Street. A string of police cars were right behind him, until Bam, Odie, Crakk, and Dev, lowered the passenger windows, and hung the upper half of their bodies out, and started raining bullets from four SKS assault rifles at their windshields.

Lit.

Chapter Twenty-Eight

Friday.
7:02 p.m.

"My bodyguards are standing outside of the women's restroom, forbidding anyone from entering, Victoria. Get there, go to the last stall, and you'll find the kilos of coke you asked for inside of a Macy's bag. Hurry."

Victoria rose from the movie theater seat with a hurry, and began excusing herself politely as she side-stepped her way by several people, who were busy staring ahead at the larger than life, movie screen. Out of the row, Victoria let out a sigh, and began walking up the dark aisle to the double doors at the rear of the movie theater. The kilos of cocaine were for Maniac.

In exchange for his information about Rock 'n Roll Rhonda, and a definite way to cause her to lose Kyzer's support, and also put her further under the radar of police, Victoria had agreed to get Maniac a few kilos of cocaine. His idea and information was well worth the payment. Victoria had a smug look on her face as she gave Salvatore Masino's Italian bodyguards a stare, while pushing the door to the women's restroom open, and walking inside.

The heels on Victoria's Christian Louboutins clicked as she walked by each stall and squatted, before moving forward. She wanted to make sure that she was indeed alone. At the last stall, she pushed the door open and hastily grabbed the Macy's bag sitting on the lid of the toilet seat. Victoria gave the contents in the bag a quick glance, before she was drawn over to the aging beauty of her reflection in the mirror. She placed her pocketbook on the vanity, and sat the Macy's bag beside her right foot.

"Yes, darling," Victoria smiled, batting her long eyelashes at her smiling reflection. She thought of texting her bodyguards, and ordering them to bring her SUV around to the front of the South Philadelphia movie theater, but then decided that she preferred to walk around to them alone. "These legs need to stay toned for Maniac. He'll be my new puppet. Yeah, I think that'll be a good idea. If his ass'll just answer his cell phone, or respond to my fuckin' text-messages. He'll help me find Sabreena. She'll have to be my new target, since Party is dead. Sab won't—"

Victoria's thoughts stopped when she saw the reflection of two sets of sneakers slowly lowering to the floor in the two adjacent bathroom stalls behind her.

Surprise.

Rock 'n Roll Rhonda and Sabreena both came out of the bathroom stalls with their guns aimed at Victoria's chest. Victoria stared at them, unable to recognize them, because of the fake beards on their faces, and their dark sunglasses. They were dressed like the movie theater employees, and the silencers fixed on the barrels of both of their guns told the silent story of what they were there to do.

Victoria wanted to know who had sent the hitmen, and why. It was obvious to her that Salvatore Masino had crossed her for someone, and before she took her last breath, Victoria simply wanted to know who that someone was.

"Who do y'all work for?"

"Ourselves," Rock 'n Roll Rhonda and Sabreena said in unison, as they both took a step forward, and began to shoot Victoria in her face and chest. When they were done, Rock 'n Roll Rhonda went into Victoria's pocketbook and removed a bottle of perfume, and a tube of lipstick. Sabreena grabbed the handles of the Macy's bag. They both walked out of the women's restroom, with their hearts thudding in their chests, and their adrenaline pumping through their veins.

A female employee gave them both a weird stare, but looked away when someone there to see a movie approached her with a question. When she turned to see where they had went, Rock 'n Roll Rhonda and Sabreena were gone.

Chapter Twenty-Nine

Saturday.
10:44 a.m.
Rock 'n Roll Rhonda had only one Glock 45 left. She had gone through thirteen of them. After each of her shootouts, and murders, she had went somewhere to disassemble her weapons. Promptly afterwards, she had tossed some pieces of the Glocks in random places of the Delaware River, and some in the Schuylkill River. Her remaining Glock 45 was down at her side, gripped firmly in her right hand, as she stared at one of the factory's surveillance monitors in the office.

There was a young woman at the factory's front door, knocking incessantly with one hand, while using her other hand to wipe away tears from her face. She appeared to be Mexican or Puerto Rican, and whenever she would turn her face to look at the passing traffic on Cecil B. Moore Avenue, bruises on the left side of her face and neck, were clearly visible. The woman was scared of someone, and for some reason the woman seemed to believe that safety was there at the factory.

Rock 'n Roll Rhonda had her own problems, and made up her mind to go and confront the young woman, knocking at the factory's door. It was her final day at the factory, and she needed to be there to wrap up her last order of murder.

The police cameras had captured the entire incident the prior night, from start to finish. Nine people had been shot, eight of them had suffered fatal gunshot wounds. Maniac had been the lone survivor. He had been rushed to a nearby hospital, where he was immediately placed in police custody. Kyzer and the Jungle Boys had gotten away. Everyone in Lil Chris' SUV had made it back to the factory, and had stuck around, until the sun had started to rise. The recorded shootout had made local and national news, and had prompted news conferences from the mayor of Philadelphia, as well as one from the police commissioner, that was currently airing live on TV. Rock 'n Roll Rhonda had been watching it on her cell phone, but was interrupted at the arrival of the woman knocking at the factory's front door.

It had been an extremely violent week. With a female cop impersonator still on the loose, and a duo of fake detectives out there, responsible for killing a real one, City Hall and police headquarters were hunting down every lead that came their way. The death of Detective Konn had many people secretly happy and relieved, on the streets of Philadelphia, and also in many of its administrative buildings.

A Philadelphia journalist had been providing the public with a lot of interesting facts about Detective Konn's past. He was the son of Detective Konn's deceased partner, and believed that his father's death had been Detective Konn's doing. All of his stories were being published in a city paper.

Victoria's death inside the women's restroom at the South Philadelphia movie theater on Columbus Boulevard had few details. A vague description of the two people of interest was given by an actual employee of the movie theater, but more attention was being given to Victoria's bodyguards, who both had been shot in the face multiple times, as they sat in the movie theater's parking lot, while watching child pornography on an iPad. The passenger had managed to crawl out of the SUV, but had died moments later beside a parked car directly next to it.

The Muslim woman that Victoria had shot, pretending to be Rock 'n Roll Rhonda had survived the attempt on her life, and she wasn't cooperating with authorities. The couple that Rock 'n Roll Rhonda had opened fire on had both died. No one in the Muslim community understood the reasons behind their tragic deaths. On social media, family members and friends were sharing stories and posting old pictures of all of the people that had died during the week. Using her fake Facebook and Instagram accounts, Rock 'n Roll Rhonda had secretly viewed it all.

"What?" Rock 'n Roll Rhonda snapped, after snatching the factory's front door open, and giving the young woman an intimidating look. The woman's blue eyes were spilling tears, as they went from hers, and down to the gun she had down at her side. "Yeah, you about to get'cha dumb ass shot. It's nobody here that can help you. Go somewhere. Bye."

"Help me, please. Please?"

"What I just say?"

"I have nowhere else to go. This– This is the only place I know."

Rock 'n Roll Rhonda gave the traffic going east and west on Cecil B. Moore Avenue a cautious look, then brought her attention back to the young woman standing in font of her. Against her better judgement, Rock 'n Roll Rhonda stepped aside, and let the distressed woman enter the factory, but never once did she remove her index finger from the trigger of her Glock. Rock 'n Roll Rhonda watched as the woman gave the inside of the factory a confused and strange look. For the first time, she noticed that the woman was barefoot.

"What's your name?"

"Eva Jimenez. I was just here two weeks ago. They lied to my family. They killed my father and brothers. My mother, too."

"Who?"

"The men that sold me and my little sister. They smuggled us here from Mexico. What happened to all of the dead bodies?"

Immigrants.

Preyed.

Upon.

2:13 p.m.

The North Philadelphia funeral home was silent, except for the occasional noise that lingered inside from the always busy, Broad Street traffic. After Storm had left the owner's office, Bam had walked out of the bathroom, nodding in grim approval at the funeral home's owner. The elderly funeral home owner was more afraid of Bam's gun, than he was of Bam himself. For Bam, it made no difference; fear was fear, on any continent in the world. Smiling, Bam sent a text-message to Rock 'n Roll Rhonda.

Rock 'n Roll Rhonda felt her cell phone vibrate in her pocket, and she was brought back to focusing on why she was inside of the coffin, holding a gun, and treating her inhales as if each one was worth a new lease on life. Before her cell phone had vibrated, she had been thinking about the day of her parents' funeral, and how sad she had felt. When her Uncle Tuna had approached her mother's coffin, while holding her, she remembered thinking to herself how the woman down in the coffin looked nothing like her mother. The same thought had come to mind when her uncle had held her over her father's coffin. She remembered the kind words her uncle had said to both of her parents, and how he had vowed to look after their daughter, as his tears had flowed down his face. It had been his vow, and his undying efforts to live up to them afterwards, that had provoked her to avenge his death.

The coffin moved and Rock 'n Roll Rhonda felt her heart pause a beat. The inside of the coffin suddenly felt like an oven. The upper half of the coffin was beginning to open, and as it did, Rock 'n Roll Rhonda also rose, bringing her gun up and pointing it at where she knew Storm would be standing.

The speed of the bullet was quicker than Storm's surprised eyes. It burned a nasty hole into the center of her forehead, and exploded out behind her left ear. She fell backwards, then down to the floor sideways, with open eyes that stared lifelessly at Rock 'n Roll Rhonda stepping over her. A second gunshot came from the funeral home's office. A moment later, Bam joined Rock 'n Roll Rhonda at the funeral home's exit, and together, they walked out, looking like a typical elderly couple.

Chapter Thirty

Sunday.
11:35 a.m.

"Whose funeral is this?"

"Remember that girl I killed at that funeral home yesterday?"

"Yeah. Wow, that was really fast."

"No, this her mother's," Rock 'n Roll Rhonda explained, while staring out of the passenger's window of the Infiniti SUV. She raised her hand to signal that she wanted Eva to slow down, as she continued to stare at all of the people filing out of the West Philadelphia church. "What the fuck?! That's Splash! Eva, slow down! How the hell he get out?! See?! Didn't I tell you?! You'll always see some fuckin' unexpected shit at a funeral. That's Splash right there with my cousin, Liberty, mom. Ain't this some shit?!"

I-95 Expressway.

Southbound.

7:52 p.m.

Rock 'n Roll Rhonda was staring thoughtfully out of the passenger's side window, as Eva, her new friend, drove in silence. They were headed to Florida, where Salvatore Masino had a place they could both relax at. The condo, he had explained, was owned by him, and was located in

Miami. Salvatore Masino had assured her that no one would know she was there.

"Eva?"

"Yes?"

"This Virginia we drivin' through. Now, look, I got more than enough money for you to check in to one of these hotels, and you'll be able to start off fresh. I'll give you twenty-five thousand."

"Rock 'n Roll, I'm staying with you. I haven't changed my mind."

"You sure?"

Eva nodded her head emphatically as she concentrated on the road ahead of her.

"Because, after I have this baby, I'm goin' back to Philly, Eva."

"I know."

"To finish doin' what I do, Eva. That guy, Splash, has to go. We about to be on vacation, but all that shit gon' end in nine months."

"I understand."

With a sigh, Rock 'n Roll Rhonda made a call on her cell phone, then placed it to her ear. As she waited for the person she was calling to answer, she stared blankly through the SUV's windshield at all of the brake lights ahead of them. Her suitcase in the backseat was full of cash, some outfits, some fake IDs, and no guns. She sat up involuntarily when the person she was calling answered.

"I thought 'chu would've been got rid of that phone. What 'chu want?"

"You not gon' believe who home."

"Who?"

"Splash."

"Yeah? Fuck 'im. Watch how quick he get parked."

"Kyzer, that's twice I showed you love, when we both know I ain't have to. The first time was when I told you to report that rental car stolen, after Jamillah shot at me, so you'd be on point, if the cops came to your house."

"Stop doin' me favors, then, if that's what 'chu call 'em."

"Kyzer?"

"What?"

"I'm not in Philly."

"Good for you."

"If that's how you see it. I'll be back in nine months. You better invest in some bulletproof helmets for you and the Jungle Boys."

"Rock 'n Roll, we wit' all the bullshit. Come through."

"I promise."

Her unborn child was his.

Their affection was once true.

But now, they were enemies.

Sneak Read of . . .

GOSSIP ALLEY

Coming Soon In 2018

Chapter One

After Monica Finley found a parking space on her grandparent's quiet, Northeast Philadelphia block, she killed the engine on her car and released an anxious sigh. As she reached into the backseat to grab her pocketbook, her boyfriend took his eyes off of the screen of his cell phone and glanced out of the passenger window.

It was dark outside, and snowing. Christmas was only three days away, and their anniversary of being a couple for a complete year was on New Year's Eve. Monica and her boyfriend, Rob, had both overcome a lot of relationship obstacles in 2014.

"Thank you for comin' over here with me."

"I only came to avoid an argument, Monica. I still don't understand why you want me here, though."

"For support."

"Monica, I'm ya fuckin' boyfriend. Just ya fuckin' boyfriend. What me being in there gon' do? This a fuckin' drug intervention. This a situation for ya mom."

"As my boyfriend, why can't 'chu see it as a situation for me?"

"So, ya family can be givin' me funny looks, like they always do? I can be at the fuckin' studio."

"Rob, I'm not doin' this wit 'chu right now," Monica argued, as she bit back the angry words that she really wanted to express. Her heart was in high hopes of her family's surprise intervention for her mother being successful, and there was nothing else today, more important, or vital, than that. "I can't. Sometimes, you just don't get it. Rob, you not here for my family. You here for me. Is that too much to ask? Am I like this when you ask for my support? I pay for your studio time. I'm at all of your shows. I got all the girls at the club, promotin' your music on their pages. Rob, I put up with so fuckin' much, and we both know it. When you found out my mom knew how to sing, didn't I go find her, and brung her to that fuckin' studio for you? Rob, most nights, I give you all of my money, after shakin' my fuckin' ass at that damn club. For your career, not mine. Rob, the least you could do, is be by my side in there, while I try to convince my mom to go into rehab. Let today be about me for once, and not the fuckin' studio."

Monica climbed out of her car with an attitude and slammed the door behind her. The evening sky above her was sprinkling thick snow flakes, and the air around her was cold and unsettling. Monica fought back tears as she trudged up the sidewalk to her grandparent's house through the ankle-length snow. One of the teardrops managed to escape from her left eye when she heard the passenger door of her car being slammed behind her. Her boyfriend's presence at her mother's intervention was extremely important to her, and in her heart, important for their relationship. Monica desperately wanted her mother to get help for her drug and alcohol addiction. This strong urge was more for her younger brother and sister, than it was for herself.

In Monica's own opinion, she was doing very well for herself. She was twenty-seven, had no children, owned her home, and was only a few hundred dollars shy of having thirty-one thousand dollars in her bank account. Monica was a successful, exotic dancer, and she was smart with her money. She had almost everything in life she had ever dreamed of, and hoped for. Her only absences of happiness came from her mother's alcohol and drug addiction, not being married, and not having any children.

Holding hands, Monica and her boyfriend walked into Monica's grandparent's house. Their appearance immediately caused mixed reactions from Monica's family members as they joined everyone in the living room. Some family members started smiling, and some were looking at the two of them with judging eyes. Monica went straight over to the sofa, where her grandparents were sitting, and gave them both warm hugs. Afterwards, ignoring the judging eyes, coming from two of her aunts, and three of her female cousins, she gave big smiles to the family members that had shown her smiling faces first. Her boyfriend pulled out his cell phone and put his back against her grandparent's basement door, quickly tuning out everyone there. It bothered Monica that he hadn't been polite enough to at least speak to her grandparents.

Monica sat between her younger brother and sister on a couch, facing her grandparents. Them, and everyone else watched as Tanya, Monica's mother, came walking into the house moments later. She had a can of beer in one hand, and a lit cigarette in the other. Monica's mother was mumbling something under her breath, until she raised her head and looked left into the living room.

Interventions.

Monica chose to speak to her mother last. Unlike her family members, her plea to her mother wasn't written on a piece of paper. She had hers memorized, and she was going to let her heart control what she wanted to say to her mother. The only dry eyes in her grandparent's living room, belonged to Monica's boyfriend. He hadn't looked up from his cell phone once.

"Mom, we, um, we all love you," Monica began, staring into her mother's crying eyes. Her own eyes were pouring tears, and the tearful pleas her younger brother and sister had made alone, had melted their mother down to her knees in front of them. "All of us do. Growin' up, you always told me I was your best friend. I always felt better and special when you would tell me that. Mom, I gotta say this, and this ain't to hurt your feelings. I got enough friends. I need a mom. You heard what Heemy and Shay just told you. We just want our mom in our lives. We all want 'chu to get help. Please?"

Despite her drug and alcohol addiction, Monica's mother was still remarkably attractive. She was forty-two, with gray eyes, and had the body of a young woman in her mid-twenties.

"Okay, I'll go to a rehab. It'll have to be in seven months."

"Mom, I'm payin' for it. You don't–Wait. Why in seven months?"

"I'm two months pregnant."

"What? By who?"

"Him."

Everyone in the living room followed the direction of where Monica's mother was pointing her finger. It was the first and only time that Monica's boyfriend looked up from his cell phone. Monica's grandmother let out a loud gasp.

"Monica, Rob got me pregnant. We fucked at the studio when I did that song with him. The baby his."

About The Author

KHALIL MURRAY was born and raised in Philadelphia Pennsylvania. Next on Khalil Murray's agenda is to turn the novels from his 10-book series, into a web-series, as well as taking the time to publish some other aspiring authors. The Equal Team Publications is always looking for new book cover models; male and female, as well as graphic designers, music producers, rap and R&B artists, and film directors.

For previews of upcoming books and projects by Khalil Murray, and more information about The Equal Team Publications, visit:

Facebook/Khalil Murray
Facebook/The Equal Team Publications
Instagram/Khalil_Murray

I'm always getting a lot of questions from dudes in jail, regarding the steps it'll take to get their books published, or how to do it themselves. I'll provide you with all the game I learned, and give you what I know at no cost. Holla at me:

Khalil Murray #HV-8680
SCI-Graterford
P.O. Box 244
Graterford, PA 19426

www.ingramcontent.com/pod-product-compliance
Lightning Source LLC
Chambersburg PA
CBHW070111260626
47160CB00004B/1414